D1647192

CLASH

LEABHARLANN
CO. CILL DARA

DERMOD JUDGE

The Book Guild Ltd

First published in Great Britain in 2017 by
The Book Guild Ltd
9 Priory Business Park
Wistow Road, Kibworth
Leicestershire, LE8 0RX
Freephone: 0800 999 2982
www.bookguild.co.uk
Email: info@bookguild.co.uk
Twitter: @bookguild

Copyright © 2017 Dermod Judge

The right of Dermod Judge to be identified as the author of this work has been asserted by him in accordance with the Copyright, Design and Patents Act 1988.

All rights reserved. No part of this publication may be reproduced, transmitted, or stored in a retrieval system, in any form or by any means, without permission in writing from the publisher, nor be otherwise circulated in any form of binding or cover other than that in which it is published and without a similar condition being imposed on the subsequent purchaser.

This work is entirely fictitious and bears no resemblance to any persons living or dead.

Typeset in Minion Pro

Printed and bound in Great Britain by CPI Group (UK) Ltd, Croydon, CR0 4YY

ISBN 978 1912083 879

British Library Cataloguing in Publication Data.
A catalogue record for this book is available from the British Library.

MIX
Paper from responsible sources
FSC® C013604
FSC www.fsc.org

This book is dedicated to the one person who thought I had stamina, the energy, the creative ability and the required years to write a novel – me.

1

"Pull on it. Like you were pulling a Presbyterian off your mother!"

The shout echoed dully around the hurling field in Kerry. The shouter was Joe Crosby, a long-armed, long-backed man in his sixties who was striding up and down the sideline in a rage.

"Will you look at the dirty eejit! He couldn't knock snow off a rope. Will you hit the bloody thing. Bigob, you're no flesh of mine."

The grinning object of this abuse was his nephew, John-Joe Crosby who was literally running rings around the rest of the players. His long, lazy lope carried him away from his pursuing opponents with ease. He flicked the ball from his hurley into the air and as it descended, sent it whistling into the goal.

He acknowledged the congratulations of his teammates and stood, breathing easily, waiting for the ball to come back into play. At twenty-five he was in his physical prime, happy to be doing what he loved best – playing the game that had dominated his life ever since his Uncle Joe had thrust a hurley into his two-year-old hands and guided him as he hit his first ball. He glanced around at the looming Kerry hills and saw the rain moving slowly towards the field. Might just finish the game without getting drenched, he thought.

Joe Crosby was also eyeing the approaching rain as he moved next to a gaunt man in a trench coat who had been enjoying both the game and Crosby's ire.

"He has them where he wants them," The gaunt man said in a broad Northern Ireland accent.

"He hasn't got them where I want them – on their knees, saying novenas for full time."

The ball soared through the darkening air and John-Joe ran to intercept it. Leaping high, he snagged it on his stick and, tapping as he ran, dodged through the clump of players who rushed at him. Emerging out the far side of the clump, he sent the ball into the goal, the crack of the ash on the leather coinciding with the rumble of thunder from the approaching storm. The whistle blew for the end of the game and Joe Crosby turned to the gaunt man.

"Didn't I tell you! The loveliest hurler in Kerry. What am I saying? In Ireland. Come over here you darlin."

Hearing the appeal, John-Joe extricated himself from his pleased teammates and disappointed opponents and ran towards them. The gaunt man spoke.

"He's everything you were in your all-Ireland days."

"Ah, I wouldn't go as far as that. You! What colour's my face?"

The question was addressed at John-Joe who ran up. He exchanged an amused glance with the gaunt man.

"Hello Uncle Joe. Mr Quirk. Blue."

"Blue!" said Crosby emphatically. "From telling you to keep those elbows in. You were flapping them around like a hen trying to lay a table. Keep them elbows in and you'll slide through them like shit through a goose. Now go and get changed and we'll see you at Malone's."

As the first raindrops started to fall John-Joe ran off after his teammates. He caught up with one of his teammates who nodded towards Joe.

"What's he giving out about now?"

"The elbows."

"Jaysus! He's never satisfied."

"Nor should he be."

"I suppose not. He got my Da as far as the all-Ireland"

"How were *his* elbows?"

"His elbows were all right, except when they were resting on a bar at the pub"

"Yes. I remember. Pity."

"It was. Your Uncle Joe had his work cut out to keep him in shape. But after that final… well… he just lost it all."

The team entered the breeze-block changing rooms as the purple slopes began to disappear in the rain. John-Joe stopped and looked out over the mountains to where the sun had given up the struggle with the low-slung dirty blue and dull violet sheet of clouds and left the slopes to an increasingly purple darkness. It was going to be a long time before he stood among the rocky protuberances of Kerry again, where the spirit of his race imbued the land with an indelible sense of rightness. Was he going to lose it all? Was he going to be swept up in the tumult of the capital city and lose touch with what was fast making him Kerry's favourite son? Its hero in the making? Its champion hurler? Sometimes, it was a burden, this hope vested in and foisted on him, this facility with the caman and the sliotar, the implements with which the ancient heroes proved their supremacy? Like Setanta – Cúchulainn, the hound of Culainn – who had to spend the growing-up period of a young pup as a guard dog – the occupation of that pup's sire – because he, Setanta, had slammed a sliotar down its throat as it attacked him. He'd been brought up on tales like that, half-believed legends and mist-enshrouded myths that would probably never die. Well he, John-Joe would slam his sliotar down Dublin's throat and live as a dog if needs be until he lived up to the expectations of his Uncle Joe and all the other grizzled, untidy, hard-living Kerrymen whose hopes of glory were riding on him; a damp, cold hurley player in a rough field at the arse end of Ireland. Christ! He could do with a pint.

Across the pitch, Crosby and Quirk pulled their coat collars up and moved towards the cars that were parked nearby.

"It's a pity John-Joe has to play on such a lousy bit of ground," said Quirk, reaching for his keys.

"There's more pitches promised. And better facilities."

"Promised! They've been promising for years. It's a wonder the young fellows bother to show up for the weekly matches."

"And why wouldn't they? They're not here to be cosseted."

"Who's said anything about cosseted! Looked after, that's all. A warm shower after a match wouldn't spoil them. A little respect is all"

"Respect! They'll get that on the pitch. But they have to earn it."

"You're a hard man, Joe Crosby."

"It's a hard game."

"There's not another like it."

Crosby grunted an assent as they climbed into the back seat of Quirk's car, an enormous Mercedes with dark windows.

"Malone's." Quirk ordered the driver, a thick-set man with black hair curling around the powerful fingers that gripped the steering wheel. He was one of the interchangeable men that Quirk always had around. They were all taciturn and powerful looking and they kept themselves very much to themselves, leaving Quirk's sprawling estate very seldom. There was much talk about them in the area but things being what they were up in Northern Ireland and Quirk being known for his extreme nationalistic views, the talk was subdued and measured.

"And the game will be ruined if that man Curran has his

way," Quirk continued as the car moved through the rain and across the grass towards the road.

"Maybe you're right."

"Of course I'm right. Curran just wants to make money. The way Packer made money out of cricket."

"But you're talking about cosseting—"

"I didn't say cosseting. You brought it up. I said respect. Asking them to turn up in a bloody field every Saturday – and for practice every Wednesday night– with no support. And very little training"

Crosby turned toward him stifling a snarl.

"Hold on to your temper," said Quirk. "They're lucky to have you as a trainer. But—"

"And a club manager too."

"And a club manager, I know, but face it, Joe, you're getting on in years. Out in all weather. How long can you go on? And who'll replace you?"

Crosby looked at the rain as it started to pour down the window.

"And who's training the trainers?" Quirk continued. "And how many would want to do what you're doing anyway? For fuck all thanks."

They were both silent as the car made its way into the village and drew up outside one of the six pubs on the main street. The rain grew heavier and the wind swept down from the hills in unexpected gusts.

Malone's could have been designed by the nineteenth century temperance champion, Father Theobald Mathew, as a deterrent to drinking and an incentive to take the pledge and wear the Pioneer pin as the badge of total abstinence. It was low-ceilinged, dark and draughty and the grime of generations coated the walls which boasted dim, branded mirrors and mildewed photographs of hurling teams. Crosby featured in several of the pictures, having risen through the various levels of the game until he had reached – and captained – the Kerry team in the all-Ireland finals three years running. Hurling had been, and still was, his life, apart from a small market-gardening business which brought in an income sufficient for his modest needs. Having coached the Kerry team for six years, he now coached half the hurling teams in the county, making him a popular man, despite his short fuse with any player whom he considered wasn't giving his best at all time. He believed the entire seventy minutes of a match, any match, should be played with total concentration and unremitting fury. It was how he had played and it was a tribute to his inherent humanity that the fury never once spilled over into foul play. He had been a tough opponent but a fair one.

The owner of the pub finished pulling three pints and put them on the bar.

"How's the team shaping up?" he asked.

"Not bad at all," said Joe as he carried his pint to his lips. "They're a good crowd of lads. They'll do well."

The owner watched the two of them drink.

"Pity John-Joe is off to Dublin," he said. "They'll miss him. We all will."

The owner moved away down the bar.

"I suppose Curran's trainers will be in clover," said Crosby.

"Yes. They're flocking to him. Have you been approached at all?"

"He knows full well what answer he'd get."

"You don't want the game changed, do you?"

"Well… they've made changes over the years. Small ones. To make it a bit safer for the players, mostly."

"Curran wants to make it more dangerous."

"Where'd you hear that?"

"I've been on his tail for years now. Ever since he started to build that new stadium of his."

"More dangerous?"

"You don't watch television do you?"

"Don't have time."

"Well if you did, you'd be shocked."

"I hear it's all sex now."

"Sex is not the problem. It's the violence. They say there's a thousand ways to kill a man and they must be near that score now."

"Ah, but that's all make believe. Special effects and things. So I hear."

"There's more than that happening. Reality TV they call it. They take real people off the street and put them in life-threatening situations. To see how they cope."

"Well?"

"The more danger, the higher the ratings."

Crosby paused the glass on the way to his lips. "Ratings?"

"Viewership," continued Quirk. "The number of people watching. The more danger there is, the more people watch. It's a pornography – of violence. And Curran is going to cash in on that."

"How?"

"By making the game violent, bloody and dangerous."

"Yes. I've heard rumours—"

"They're not rumours. They're facts. I've sent men to watch his training sessions. They have doctors in attendance – all the time. And those who drop out because of the violence are paid to keep their mouths shut. Or scared."

"Well, you'd know about that. Secrecy and violence. It's not a troupe of boy scouts you have up there at your place."

Quirk pauses in his drinking.

"If anyone else had said that…"

"Ah, come on! My whole family has blood on their hands. Since way back. But that was for a cause"

Quirk sipped his drink.

"A cause, yes. It's still there," he said.

"So you say. Is anybody interested any more?"

"Oh yes."

They both drank silently.

Quirk and he were friends, in spite of their totally different backgrounds and temperaments. Where Crosby was quick to speak his mind, Quirk was careful and circumspect. Where Crosby was straightforward in all his beliefs and actions, Quirk was devious. Where Crosby's nationalism was uncomplicated and traditional, Quirk's was fanatical. While Crosby saw a fully united Ireland as a slow but historic inevitability, Quirk was widely known to be involved in bringing it about in ways that frightened many people North and South of the border. What had brought them together was love of hurling but even here, their attitudes to the game varied, Crosby perceived it as the supreme physical challenge while Quirk regarded it as the defining expression of Ireland's ancient glory and destiny.

Crosby and Quirk had finished their pints when John-Joe burst in through the pub door in a miasma of rain, wind and bustling energy. He was greeted by several people who were standing around and he stopped to talk to them. Crosby indicated the pint standing on the smeared bar to the owner.

"Top that up will you. And two more."

John-Joe left the group and joined them, taking off his jacket and shaking it. The owner placed the topped-up pint on the counter.

"How's it going there?" he asked.

"It's good. It's good," replied John-Joe. "Apart from the rain."

"Ah sure, we need it." The owner moved away. "Get outside of that," said Crosby. "It'll keep off the chill."

"Thanks," said John-Joe, burying his upper lip and nose in the glass. The others watched the absorption of the stout with approval.

"Bigob," said Crosby. "I could hear that hitting the bottom of your belly."

"You did some nice stuff out there," said Quirk.

"And why not?" expostulated Crosby. "Sure he wasn't stretched."

John-Joe placed the severely-diminished pint on the bar and grinned at Quirk. The owner placed two more pints on the bar.

"Maybe you think I wasn't stretched because I make it look so easy," he said.

"The day you think hurling's easy..." Crosby started, rising to the bait.

"Easy yourself, Crosby. He's pulling your leg," said Quirk. "He respects the game and the skills required to play it as much as you do. Am'n't I right, John-Joe?"

John-Joe nodded and attacked the pint again.

"When are you off to Dublin?" asked Quirk, taking a more moderate sip of his drink.

"Tomorrow. A transfer. God knows why. Any civil servant in Ireland could do what I'm doing."

"That's the civil service for you – a meat grinder. It takes in young men and grinds out old farts. But it's no matter. I think it's an opportunity for you to find out about Curran and that *Danann* team of his."

"I'm not so sure about that," said Crosby. "I'm told he's on the lookout for the best players in the country, but I'm not sure you should get involved with him."

"Now Joe, we agreed John-Joe should at least look around."

"We did. But a look around is all we ask. Join a club. I'm sure he'll find you."

"I'm not sure I'll want to be found. I hear he's turning the game on its head."

"He is. And he's being very secretive about it," said Quirk. "That's why you should have a look."

"OK. I will."

"Look," said Crosby laboriously. "You're a level-headed fellow and you love the game. You'd be hard to turn."

"Find out what you can," said Quirk. "Look around. Keep your eyes open. OK?"

John-Joe took a long pull on his pint.

"OK," he said finally.

The next pints were downed to the sounds of Crosby and Quirk offering advice to John-Joe about hurling, living in Dublin and diverse matter pertaining to keeping his nose clean and his eye on the ball generally.

"And the girls now," said Crosby, after a long pause. John-Joe pretended not to have heard. He pulled on his pint and looked around at the several badly-dressed men in the pub. Bachelors to a man, he guessed, like his uncle who was notoriously shy around females and was reputed never to have touched a woman in his life. An unusual reputation, even in this semi-celibate country.

"Did you hear me now?" Crosby asked. Quirk turned his head away in disapproval and John-Joe smiled at his uncle.

"Uncle Joe. I was a quarter-of-a-century old in January. So I think—"

"Age has nothing to do with it."

"What then?"

Crosby blushed, obviously sorry he had embarked on such a treacherous sea. He took up his pint and examined it carefully.

"Just so's you understand and… and… and you're careful. Three more pints there?" he bellowed at the owner, as if it was all his fault.

2

Dublin had changed in the three years since he had been there. It was brasher. There were more impressive cars on the clogged roads. The young people carried themselves with a swagger. The city was cleaner than he remembered and bigger. Down by the docks, a cluster of high-rise office blocks had appeared from nowhere and smartly-dressed men and women ran up and down the steps, whirred through the revolving doors and ducked across the broad pavements with a haste and determination he'd never seen before.

He had left his suitcase at the bus station and was wandering, hurley in his grip, around the south side of the city, over the Liffey, enjoying the bustle and admiring the girls, many of whom grinned back when he sent out admiring signals. He was stopped in his tracks by an enormous TV set in a shop window. There were large speakers suspended outside the shop through which the soundtrack came blaring. On the screen was hurling like he'd never seen it. It was a brutal, violent and superb television commercial, a mixture of slow motion and speeded up action, all synchronised with a pounding music track. Sound effects were interspersed; the thud of bodies, the crack of stick and ball, the grunts of the players and the gasps and cheers of the crowd. The players were all dressed in sleek, tight uniforms, stretching smoothly down to the metallic boots and the top part had the *Danann* logo emblazoned on the front.

Zapping across the screen were the words; "The *Danann* are coming." Suddenly a man's face appeared on the screen. Superimposed was his name: Jack Curran.

"I promise you action. I promise you danger," he rasped. "I promise you the game that will define sport for the next hundred years."

Then, over a computer-generated graphic of an enormous sports stadium, the voice over declaimed: "Arena21 is almost ready. It's forty-five days to the first match. The world will be watching. Will you?"

It was like the trailer for a Kung Fu movie and John-Joe was stunned. He hefted the hurley in his hand and wagged it slowly from side to side.

Two passing men noticed this.

"Another big ignorant culchie," muttered one.

"Yeh. With stars in his fucking eyes."

John-Joe ignored them. Curran was being interviewed.

"Mr Curran, you have been accused of trying to destroy hurling by commercialising it, making it totally professional," the earnest interviewer, with a black wire spiralling out from behind his ear, asked.

"The so-called purists tried to prevent professionalism at Wimbledon but look how tennis has thrived since then," replied Curran. "And see how much more exciting cricket became since Kerry Packer put it on a more professional level. In hurling, Ireland has the fastest stick and ball game on the planet. Through the *Danann*, the most formidable team ever seen in sport, I intend to share hurling with the world."

John-Joe couldn't help it. He had to see Arena21, the much-vaunted sports stadium built by Jack Curran at enormous expense and in highly controversial circumstances. Bribery and corruption rumours about the granting of planning permission had buzzed around Ireland at the time. There was even talk, at one stage, of Arena21 becoming the home of Irish hurling, instead of the traditional Croke Park in North Dublin. An official of the ruling body, the Gaelic Athletic Association, had resigned under a cloud after making suggestions to that effect.

It took half an hour to get to Arena21 by bus and he walked around the bustling but nearly-completed building with its severe security, its high-rise office block and the enormous poster advertising the *Danann*. High above the site, a dirigible was tethered with a spherical electronic counter suspended beneath. This was a day-by-day countdown to the opening. Cranes swooped, cement mixers thundered and hundreds of construction workers clambered over and around every slab of cement, face panel of aggregate and pane of glass.

John-Joe walked to the bottom of the steps leading to the office block. It soared above him, marble, steel and glass glinting in the early evening sun. It looked more like the headquarters of an international banking group than a sports arena and John-Joe was appropriately intimidated.

One security guard, seeing him with his hurley, beckoned him to approach. John-Joe grinned and shook his head, turning away in deep thought. It was dark in the street and he suddenly realised that he was on the far side of the city from the residence organised for him by Uncle Joe, through the network of Kerry expatriates.

When he arrived back in Oxmantown Road, the long street stretched away into the darkness. Pools of light from the row of lampposts illuminated the double storey houses on either side. He peered at the number on the nearest door; 261 – and he wanted number 19. Hitching his bag over his left arm and his suitcase on his left shoulder, he set off into the dwindling perspective. There were few cars on the road, the celebrated economic miracle of Dublin hadn't penetrated this section.

Suddenly a surge of excitement ran through him. He was on his own in the capital, a new job awaited, which he knew he could more than cope with, and sporting possibilities loomed that could fuel his love of exercise and competition. He had been charged to look into the *Danann* but that would wait. He had Dublin to experience. He slipped a ball out of his pocket and balanced it on the hurley. Tapping it up and down, he created a four-to-the-bar rhythm and started to move his feet in time to it. He had always excelled at Irish dancing and was proud of his lightness of foot. Up he went on his toes and did a pretty deft reel down the middle of the street.

He managed to keep the ball on the hurley for almost the full length of the street before it slipped off and rolled under a small car parked by the kerb. He lowered his bag and suitcase onto the path and looked at the number on the door. No. 19. The ball had rolled against the kerb and he gave a final rat-tat-tat with his feet and bent down to retrieve it. Suddenly from the car came a laughing voice raised in song;

"*Oh the days of the Kerry dances.*"

He sat back on his heels in embarrassment. A pretty face loomed out of the open car window on a level with his.

"John-Joe Crosby, I presume?"

"How'd you know that?"

"It wasn't easy working it out. Dublin's full of eejits hurling and hopping down the streets in the middle of the night, looking for Mrs Ring's house."

"So this is Mrs Ring's house?"

"Good guess, JJ. And I'm Kitty Ring."

"Hello Kitty Ring."

"If you let me out of the car I'll let you into the house."

"Sorry."

He scrambled to his feet and opened the door for her. She swung her legs out and he looked at them approvingly, a reaction she didn't miss as she wound the window closed.

He approved of the rest of her, too as she strode across the pavement and opened the door to number nineteen. She was beautiful in a strikingly Irish way with pale skin, raven hair and bright blue eyes. She was of moderate height with a splendid body which her quietly stylish way of dressing flattered. John-Joe followed her into the house, feeling very much at peace with the world.

Kitty put her fingers on her lips and closed the door gently. From the back room came a sweet, slightly uncertain voice.

"*Stor ma chroi*
When you're far away
From the land you'll soon be leaving
'tis many a time by night and by day
Your heart will be sorely grieving."

The old song, sung in the *sean nos* style, pleased both of them as they stood in the darkened hallway. It was the quintessential song about the quintessential Irish experience – emigration.

"How many Irish people sang that after they left home, I wonder?" whispered John-Joe, a slight lump in his throat.

"Relax, JJ, you've only come as far as Stoneybatter."

She pushed open the door and breezed into the back room.

"Another orphan of the night, Mammy."

Mrs Ring was ensconced in a huge armchair in front of a blazing fire and clutching a glass of whiskey. Next to her, in a dressing gown, was Tim Prendergast, a slim, wiry man the same age as John-Joe. He hurriedly placed the glass he was holding on the mantelpiece and leapt to his feet to greet John-Joe.

"I thought you'd never get here. What kept you? Hello Kitty.

Sorry, Mrs Ring, this is John-Joe Crosby," he presented John-Joe to Mrs Ring's gaze, with smiling pride.

"And what time does Mr John-Joe Crosby think this is?" asked Mrs Ring.

Tim was a bit put out by this lack of warmth but John-Joe was unfazed. He reached into his bag and pulled out a small bottle of colourless liquid.

"It's time for a peace offering from your home county, Mrs Ring," he said. "Tim wrote me that you had a touch of what you call the bronnical breathing."

Mrs Ring tossed back the contents of her glass and held it out to John-Joe.

"Only at night," she said.

"This is a sure cure. Made last week," said John-Joe as he poured a generous tot. "My Uncle Joe swears by it."

Mrs Ring, sipped the poteen and sighed.

"Sit down, John-Joe. It's nice to have another Kerryman staying here. We miss the place. What was it kept you?"

"I left my suitcase at the bus station and decided I wanted to see a bit of Dublin."

"Well, you're welcome to this bit of it anyway," said Mrs Ring. "We'll look after you. Tim, show John-Joe to his room. You've a lot to say to each other."

"A cup of tea and some toast'll be ready in a few minutes," said Kitty, who had started to lay the table. Tim ushered John-Joe up the stairs and into the back bedroom.

The room had a desk and floor-to-ceiling shelves at one end, all of which were laden with TV capturing and editing equipment. A small digital editing suite was set up on the desk and next to it stood a row of video tapes, a tiny but impressive digital video camera and an Apple Mac. A swivel typist's chair faced it all.

"This was Tomas's room, Kitty's brother. He was a cameraman for TV 2"

"Was?"

"He died a few months ago. Kitty nearly went to pieces. They were very close. Em... what do you think of her?"

"Don't tell me you set your cap at Kitty? What would she want with a man who wears his coat in the house?"

"By Jesus!" said Tim in a thick Kerry accent. "You can take the boy out of Kerry but you can't take Kerry out of the boy."

"What have you been doing in Dublin?"

"Well, I joined a club. We play every Saturday. You must join."

"I will. And work?"

"Work, is it? Work is work. I get through the day. I get paid on the twenty-fifth of every month. I go to a dance every Saturday too. Kitty comes with me sometimes."

"Are you and her...?"

"Not really. I'd like to but she's... em... well, she's a Dublin girl and they're full of shite."

"What does she do?"

"She works in a graphics company. Drives her own car. She'd live in her own flat if it wasn't for her mother."

"Are these good digs?"

"The best you'll get in Dublin. Good food. Not too far from town. Near the Park, where we play. We better get down. Kitty said she'd make us some toast."

Kitty had made some toast and a pot of strong tea. They took their places at the table and smeared a generous helping of butter over the crisp bread while Kitty plied the toasting fork over the embers. The smell of toast and tea was soothing. Mrs Ring finished her drink and heaved herself to her feet.

"Well, I'm off," she said. "Don't keep Kitty up too late, she has a job to go to in the morning." To John-Joe she said "Sorry about the tea."

They all chorused good night and she moved into the hallway and then into the front room. They sat in companionable silence until the front-room door closed. John-Joe poured himself another cup of tea and then spoke.

"What's that about the tea? There's nothing wrong with it."

"Oh I broke her old teapot, a brown one with a dribbling spout. It was my grandmother's and she brought it here from Kerry. She always said the secret of a good cup of tea is the pot. She'd never let me wash it, only rinse it with water to flush out the tea leaves. When it broke, I found the inside caked with tannin inches thick, years and years of it. This pot is the same size and it holds six cups. The old one only held four. Tea will never be to her liking until the tannin's as thick inside this pot as was in the old one."

Kitty blushed.

"There. I'm babbling."

"Well I tend to agree with your mother," said John-Joe. "There's nothing like archaeological layers of tannin to give tea a good flavour. I hope you don't mind me sleeping in your brother's room?"

Tim's intake of breath drew Kitty's attention.

"It's all right Tim, I don't mind talking about Tomas. In fact I'm upset at the way people avoid talking about him," she turned to John-Joe. "I'm going to find out who killed him."

"Killed?"

"Oh yes. He was killed all right. He… He was found in his car in the Liffey. All the windows were open and his gear was there but not the bag for notes and his video cards, he carried that everywhere. He was onto something big. He always got secretive when he was close to something really important. Otherwise he told us everything."

"What do you think it was?"

"Some big government project. Some story on corruption."

Tim spoke up.

"You've no idea how much corruption there is in this city. Every bloody politician seems to have his hands dirty.

"Fumbling in a greasy till," said John-Joe.

"What?"

"Nothing. A poem."

"It's become a joke with Dubliners," continued Tim.

"Only it's no joke when they start killing journalists who are asking too many questions," said Kitty as she started another piece of toast.

"You've no idea what it was about?"

"Not yet."

"Is there anything on the tapes up there?"

"He was using cards to record on. No, nothing on them."

"Kitty's been through them all," said Tim.

"All that's in this house, anyway," said Kitty. "Tomas was like a magpie. He kept everything but there's a card missing."

"How do you know?"

"When he bought his new camera he bought a box with four cards with it and we can only find three. Once I find that card, I'll know what the story was and I'll know who killed him."

The toast burst into flame.

"And then I'll make them pay," Kitty said, flicking the burning bread onto the embers. "It's late. I'm off to bed."

She rose to her feet and the two men rose also.

"Now that's a sight you seldom see in Dublin. Goodnight boys."

"Good night."

"Sleep well."

She left. Tim reached across and took half a slice of toast off John-Joe's plate.

"Hey!"

"Oh stop moaning. How's the hurling back in Kerry?"

"It's all right. But it's a long time since I had a really hard game. You get a little tired of winning."

"*You* do.

"How's your club? Any chance of it getting into the provincial finals?"

"A good chance, if you join."

"What's the competition like?"

"It's getting interesting, now that we've worked our way up. We play the county winners next."

"When are you playing next?"

"Saturday."

"Good. Tell me about Curran."

"That bastard. He's going to ruin the game. And that fucking stadium—"

"Yes. I saw it this afternoon."

"You went there? Why?"

"To see it."

"And?"

"It's going to be amazing. Last Saturday I played a match on a lousy field in Kerry, with a 'changing room' you wouldn't keep a self-respecting cow in. That's got to stop. What's the word on Curran at the club?"

"That he's going to ruin the game."

"How exactly?"

"First of all by commercialising it."

"Would that be such a bad thing?"

"How can you say that?"

"I love the game and I hate my job," said John-Joe. "Nothing would suit me better than to play as a professional. Earn a living from it for a few years and then move into training. Make a lifetime job out of it. Like the soccer players in England and the tennis players everywhere."

"The GAA is totally against—"

"I know. They want 'volunteers' who'll play for the love of it"

"And what's wrong with that?"

"And what's wrong with me wanting to make a living out of it? Things are changing in sport everywhere. I just think that hurling should keep up. Not get stuck in some glorious image of the past. Look at Uncle Joe. He gave his life for the game and what thanks does he get? A lousy stipend that wouldn't keep him in pints."

"So you'd turn pro?"

"Yes. Just like the tennis and soccer players."

"You'd join the *Danann*?"

"I don't know about that. I'm certainly going to have a look. Uncle Joe asked me to anyway. And Quirk."

"Now there's a dangerous man."

"He was reared in a dangerous world. He's just a little out-of-date in his thinking. Like the GAA. Tim, professionalism won't destroy hurling. It'll grow the game. Like it grew tennis and soccer."

"I can't say I agree with you. You'll come on Saturday?"

"Yes."

"And join?

"We'll see."

3

The following Saturday, John-Joe and Tim walked up to the end of Oxmantown Road, with its interminable row of cramped, two-storey, brick housing where the earlier inhabitants used to wash the pavements outside their houses once a week, onto the well-wooded North Circular road lined with imposing three-storey houses boasting a wide set of steps up to the first floor. Under the closely-spaced plane trees they walked until the entered the Phoenix Park through the iron gates. Each of them had a tog bag slung over their shoulder and each clutched a hurley. Some rooks grumbled in the trees as they passed the Wellington Monument and approached the playing fields on the fifteen acres, under the loom of the huge cross set up for the visit of Pope Paul II. It was an overcast day and the cloud cover dulled the colour of the grass and the trees. The shouts of players of all ages grew louder.

"Hasn't this team of yours got its own grounds?" asked John-Joe.

"There's few enough teams with that sort of money."

"Curran says he has plans to build proper facilities all over."

"I'll believe that when I see it. Anyway, the goughers would be into them too. Just like the stadium. Jesus. The bribes that changed hands there."

John-Joe slipped a ball out of his pocket and threw it ahead of them. They both raced after it.

"He's recruiting, isn't he?"

"He's looking for bowsies. Thugs who don't give a damn about the game."

John-Joe got to the ball first and stood over it, effortlessly blocking every effort of Tim's to hit it with his stick.

"I don't know," said John-Joe. "It sounds pretty exciting."

"He'll ruin the game. Turn it into a bloody spectacle for sadists," said Tim, giving up trying to touch the ball and walking ahead.

"Where's this bloody pitch of yours?" said John-Joe, bouncing the ball on his hurley as he followed.

They reached the pitch and John-Joe was introduced to the team. Many of them had heard of him and expressed their pleasure as they welcomed him. It was a warm-up game for an inter-club match they needed to win in order to stay in the round of matches which led up to the inter-county games in two months' time. In the draughty breeze-block changing room, as they were tying their boots, John-Joe asked a question of the team.

"Has anybody seen the *Danann* play?"

Nobody had.

"He's keeping their style a secret until the first match," said Tim.

"Against the rest of Ireland," volunteered a player.

"Who will they be?" enquired John-Joe.

"A Dublin man called Duggan is putting that team together."

"Where would I find this Duggan?" asked John-Joe.

There was an embarrassed silence, broken by the referee who stuck his head around the door.

"Come on, lads. Let's get started," he called.

They filed out onto the pitch where the other team was taking up their positions. Tim walked next to John-Joe.

"You'd never play for Duggan?"

"Why not?"

"Jesus. I'd rather play for the *Danann*."

"Now *that* money must be good," said John-Joe. Tim was about to explode when the whistle blew for the match to start. John-Joe played with his usual dedication and energy and this was not overlooked by an immaculately-dressed man who approached the field during the second half as John-Joe scored the winning goal for his team. He watched the natural dominance that John-Joe demonstrated over all the other players and the way that his teammates automatically responded to his shouted instructions. Tim was very responsive to his needs and his playing and scored several points from the passes that John-Joe fed him as well as the opportunities that John-Joe created for him. As for the two men who tried to mark him as soon as they saw his capabilities, John-Joe was forever outwitting them, never being where they expected him to be and moving in directions they could never accurately anticipate. All in all, it was John-Joe's game and Tim basked in his reflected glory.

Later in the afternoon John-Joe and Tim were walking home along the main road through the park and reliving the match.

"Jesus! The way you got through that scrimmage! They never knew you were there."

"It's all to do with the elbows."

A gleaming dark-blue Rover drew level with them, on the wrong side of the road, so that the driver's window was next to them as it opened silently. The immaculately-dressed man was driving.

"John-Joe Crosby. Welcome to Dublin. The city of opportunity."

"For who, exactly?" asked Tim warily.

"For those with highly-marketable skills and outstanding abilities."

He reached out his arm and offered a business card to John-Joe, who stepped over and took it as the car stopped.

"Pat O'Shea. *Danann* scout," read John-Joe.

"We want nothing to do with you," said Tim angrily.

"I'm interested in John-Joe, providing John-Joe is interested in earning big money doing what he does better than any hurler I've seen in action this year."

"Well, John-Joe is not interested," said Tim.

"I'll believe John-Joe is not interested when I hear John-Joe say he's not interested."

They both looked at John-Joe who remained silent.

"You know it breaks my heart," said O'Shea "seeing talent like you walking home from a hard match, when you could be driving home in a car like this."

John-Joe reached out and wiped a piece of dirt off the bonnet of the Rover. It was almost a caress.

"Hop in," said O'Shea. "I'll drop you home."

John-Joe slowly brushed the dirt off his hand before replying.

"No thanks. We've got someplace to go."

"OK. Keep the card. Give us a call if you want to see what we're up to."

The window slid up and the car moved smoothly away towards the city. John-Joe pocketed the card, which action was noticed by Tim.

"Jesus, John-Joe, for a minute there—"

"You thought I'd fall for it? I'm not that green. Come on. You owe me a pint."

4

That night Tim and Kitty took John-Joe nightclubbing. They started north of the River Liffey with a substantial Chinese meal which John-Joe admitted was his first. Kitty and Tim guided him through the menu and he did it full justice as they washed it down with chilled white wine. They left the restaurant and made their way down a quiet, dimly-lit street, over the Halfpenny Bridge towards Temple Bar. They paused on the bridge and looked down on the dark, silent and swiftly flowing water. Suddenly Kitty started to sing softly

Fare thee well my Anna Liffey
I can no longer stay
And watch the new glass cages
That rise up along the quay
My mind's too full of memories
Too old to hear new chimes
I'm a part of Dublin city
In the rare ould times.

Her voice faded.

"Tomas loved that song."

"Did he now?"

"He did. He was in a group called the Anna Liffies. He played the *bodhran* and sang. A terrible voice, low and rough but great for a pub. The group came to his funeral and sang it at the graveside."

They were quiet for a while then John-Joe cupped his hands behind his ears and faced North, which was silent except for a few cars passing. He slowly turned 180 degrees South and laughed at the noise of people. Lots of people.

"God. Two different cities."

They all laughed and walked on across the bridge. As they did, John-Joe reached out, grabbed and squeezed Kitty's hand briefly before letting it go.

"Come on, JJ," she said. "It's time for your baptism."

The cobbled streets of Temple Bar were wall-to-wall with drunken, rowdy revellers. There was singing, fighting, shouting, staggering, embracing and vomiting everywhere; all the wicked wantonness that drunken humanity is heir to. Lights of many and varied hues slashed and flashed out of doorways, past the dark loom of bulky bouncers. Faces in gaping disarray passed in and out of the different shades, like the denizens of some ghastly dark Goya etching. Music crashed out of each door, oozing in a noxious exhalation through and around the reeling bodies. Voices in a tangled cacophony, rose and fell like a moral discord on the ear. Speech was impossible, screeching and shrieking was the norm and incomprehension was the order of the inebriated; inevitable and inexorable Saturday night in Dublin. John-Joe was stunned. Kitty grabbed his hand and tried to drag him towards a multi-coloured, strobing orifice in a brick wall but he was mesmerised by a man who was doubled over against a rusty corrugated iron gate, emptying his stomach of its alcoholic burden and complaining bitterly at his discomfort.

"Jaysus! Ooop Gukaken! Boh! Iiiiilaa! Christ! Uuugh... gokg... yaaaah! Fuck me! Hmmmmmn! Blady! Ikkelijk Ugh!

Whee!!!!!! Shit! Waaaaakkkkkshshshshsh! Pttooo! Klaaak! Bloody 'ell. Hoooooooie! Gaaaaarrr!!!! Phwphwphwt!"

"Pure Joyce. I never thought I'd hear it spoken' he said.

"Come on JJ. We've work to do"

She dragged him through the doorway, down some stone steps onto an open space full of reeling and shouting bodies, across to a well-stocked bar and a barman in sequins who twinkled as he dispensed drinks with abandon. He mouthed something at John-Joe.

"What?" yelled John-Joe.

"We don't serve pints," yelled the barman, pushing three cocktails at them. "There. Half price. It's happy hour. Be happy."

"What do you think this is?" asked John-Joe of Tim.

"Half price," said Tim, picking his up. All three sipped tentatively. A bare-chested, thin man in a string vest and satin pants pushed through them up to the bar.

"I never want to see you again. Never," he screamed at the oblivious barman and flounced off.

"What's in this thing?" asked John-Joe.

"It's a white Russian," said Kitty.

The barman placed a tab on a saucer and pushed it around on the bar in front of them until John-Joe picked it up.

"This is half price?" he said. The barman stood sparkling at him until he passed over some money. John-Joe looked up and down the bar and his glance fell on a plateful of dark brown slabs next to him. He took one, popped it into his mouth and chewed it.

"Weird snacks," he said, washing it down with his drink. "*Perestroika*."

The barman placed the saucer back in front of him. It had very little change on it.

"'nkew," he incandesced before pirouetting away.

The man standing next to John-Joe and pressed up against him turned to address him, a joint held delicately in his hand.

"Hey, handsome, got a light?" he asked.

John-Joe saw a book of matches on the bar, picked it up and lit the joint. The man inhaled deeply and, looking deep into John-Joe's eyes, blew the smoke into his face. John-Joe coughed and turned away to finish his drink. As he surveyed the dancing throng, the smoke from the joint drifted past and into his nostrils.

"Funny smell," he said and then knocked back the cocktail. "That White Russian wasn't bad. Let's have another," he signalled to the barman who super-novad over. "Three more, please."

"Dublin at play," said Kitty, replacing her empty glass on the bar.

"Looks like hard work to me," said John-Joe as he stifled a giggle.

Just then a muscular man in black sleeveless vest and tight-black pants approached the two men standing next to John-Joe. They both cringed a little.

"Buy you bitches a drink?" asked black vest of the two barflies.

They nodded silently as the man signalled two drinks to the barman who approached, looking very subdued. He placed the two White Russians in front of the barflies, where the man indicated and moved away without his usual glow.

"Tomorrow. Don't be late," said black vest to the grateful barflies as he turned away and caught John-Joe looking at him.

"You'll know me next fucking time, won't you?" he growled.

"If there is a next time," replied John-Joe, straightening up a little.

The man wasn't listening. He had just caught sight of Kitty who got uncomfortable under the stare and turned to the bar. The man's eyes travelled up and down her body. John-Joe was about to do something, he wasn't quite sure what, when she turned and handed him a drink. The man slouched away and John-Joe tossed his drink back just as Kitty turned to clink glasses with him.

"He was looking at your…" he said.

"My what, JJ?"

"Vinnie Murphy," Tim cut in. "Played for Leinster. They say he's joined Curran. They deserve each other."

"I know who he is," said Kitty. "He's the captain of their first team."

John-Joe suddenly felt totally uninhibited. He started to sway with the pounding music.

"Kitty," he commanded. "Let's dance."

He moved onto the dance floor and took up a highly theatrical pose. Kitty exchanged amused glances with Tim and followed him. A small man, with a drink in each hand, was trying to make his way around the dancers. He almost collided with John-Joe.

"Sorry," he said. He looked at the drinks. "Oh dear," he exclaimed.

"What's the matter, my good man?" asked John-Joe expansively.

"I've forgotten which is the brandy and which is the whiskey. She'll kill me."

"I'm an expert on both," said John-Joe, taking one glass. He drank it in one go. "That was brandy," he declared, taking the other glass, which he dispatched just as neatly. "And that was whiskey."

The man was distraught.

"She'll kill me," he said, heading back towards the bar.

John-Joe suddenly broke into a loose-limbed, hyped up version of Irish dancing. Toes and heels tapping on the ground, legs twirling, arms held at chest height, forearms upright, head held erect, moving slowly from side to side. He was very fast and very good. Kitty just stood there and looked at him until he finished.

"Now that's a sight you seldom see in Dublin," she said, laughing. "Come on. Coffee for you."

She took his arm and led him back to where Tim was watching it all in delight. Suddenly, Vinnie had Kitty by the arm.

"Buy you a drink?" he asked.

John-Joe stepped forward, so did Vinnie. They stood there, nose-to-nose.

"For God's sake," said Kitty, pushing between them. "What's wrong with the two of you? Are your trusses too tight?"

She nodded at Tim, and dragged John-Joe towards the door. Tim was hard on their heels.

"Welcome to Dublin," said Kitty as they left the nightclub.

5

Kitty took the next day off to show John-Joe Dublin.

"We've just finished a major project and we all worked hours of overtime. Unpaid, I might add, so we can take time off for the next week or so. Anyway, I like showing off the things in Dublin that appeal to me."

"What do you do, exactly?"

"I'm a graphic designer."

They were walking up Grafton Street on the way to Stephen's Green on a blustery, overcast day with promises of sunshine.

"I do computer design and illustration and I work with photographs, manipulating them and enhancing them. I studied for two years in a design school here. I can get work anywhere with my qualifications."

"So what keeps you in Dublin?"

"My mother. But maybe when she passes on I'll travel and see if the rest of the world is as screwed up as here."

"You sound so cynical."

"It's hard not to be. There's so much corruption here and a love – no, a passion – for consumption. All the fancy cars, the glitzy clothes, the enormous houses. They're all on borrowed money. All these 'Celtic tigers' are in debt."

"That makes their possession their bank manager's problems."

"My, JJ, aren't you the glib *culchie*. You'd probably join them if you could."

"Fat chance of that on a civil-servant's salary. But maybe if I join the *Danann*."

"Would you?"

"Don't know. But in a fair world I would make a lot of money as a professional player."

"So what colour would it be?"

"What?"

"The car."

"Blue. Like your eyes."

"By God. Kerrymen have come on since I was there."

"I would have thought that a Dublin *cailin* would be more gracious."

"Oh go *raibh maith agat a fir*."

"That's better."

A young, fair-haired man was singing and playing a guitar, with the guitar case open at his feet. Some coins dotted the dark blue lining of the case.

"In the merry month of May from my home I started
Left the girls of Tuam nearly broken-hearted
Saluted father dear, kissed my darlin' mother
Drank a pint of beer, my grief and tears to cover."

John-Joe threw a coin into the case which the singer acknowledged with a nod. They moved on through a small knot of tourists who stood watching the singer.

"Are you not part of the Celtic tiger?"

"Well, there's plenty of work for me anyway and the pay is good."

"What sort of design work do you do?"

"We've got several big clients. The *Danann* team is one. We do all their graphics. Brochures, logos, posters. I enjoy that."

"Oh. You like hurling?"

"Can't stand it."

"I never thought I'd hear a Ring say that."

"That's because you've only ever spoken to the men in the family. Thanks."

He had taken her arm lightly and guided her across the road with an easy, old-world courtesy.

"Hurling is part of the old Ireland that I came here to get away from," she said as they reached the sidewalk. "And here I am doing the graphics for the *Danann*!"

"What do you know about them?"

"Not a lot. But the little I know I don't like."

"Because of what they're doing to the game?"

"Not so much that. The game needs a shake up anyway. It seems to be wandering around in a Celtic twilight. My father believed that the Druids started it all. The fecking Druids. Sorry. Am I offending you?"

"No. Just because the game is important to me, it doesn't have to be important to everybody. But I sometimes feel that the game is at the same stage as the country. There are big opportunities out there in the world and we should be able to take advantage of them without losing our… souls, I suppose."

"And would you lose your soul on a hurling pitch?"

He suddenly turned serious.

"Look. I'm a good player and a lousy civil servant. I want to be a full-time player but professionalism is not allowed, so I can't make a good living, not even a decent living, at it. So, I'm stuck to a desk doing inconsequential things until I'm in my fifties, when I'll be doing things which I hope will have some consequence."

"That's the civil service for you."

"A man said that to me two days ago. He also said that it's a meat grinder. It takes in young man and grinds out old farts."

"What man was that?"

"A man you don't want to know. But you! You've got your digital passport to the world."

"I have, so."

They walked under the ornamental arch into Stephen's Green. John-Joe stopped to look at the names of Boer War battles engraved on the arch.

"I wonder how many Irishmen died in that war?" he mused.

"My grandfather's brother did. Then Granddad joined the Dublin Fusiliers when the first world war broke out but an uncle of mine joined the Irish Republican Brotherhood. It split the family."

"It split many families. Mine too. But so did the civil war – I've uncles who still don't talk to each other. Why do you like the graphics of the *Danann*?"

"They're great images to work with. Bulging muscles, purple and black uniforms, bodies flying and a very sexy type font, specially designed, a crisp uncial, like the one in the *Book of Kells* but sloping and very modern looking. That's always in gold. That's where I know Vinnie from. He modelled for the main figure but I pumped up his biceps and triceps and lengthened his legs. Made him look like Captain America on steroids. You're laughing at me."

"I'm not. I'm enjoying your enthusiasm. Will you show me the Book of Kells?"

"I will. It's in Trinity College."

They walked through the Green and had pints and sandwiches in a Baggot Street pub; great slabs of ham with mustard that made their eyes prickle. Then across to the National Gallery to see Caravaggio's *The Taking of Christ*, in front of which Kitty stood in awe.

"Will you look at that arm!" she said, indicating the mail-clad soldier reaching across the painting to grasp Christ by the throat. "It dominates the whole picture. And to think it hung for years in the J's dining room."

"J's?"

"The Jesuits. They didn't know what they were looking at."

Then it was down to Trinity College library to peer at the Book of Kells, faintly lit by a dim overhead spotlight.

"You can hardly see the bloody thing," John-Joe complained.

"They have to keep it dark. The ink and gold leaf were fading."

Dublin Castle was a surprise to John-Joe.

"I always imagined it dark and brooding, a bit like Dracula's castle."

"Well, there were some dark deeds done here."

They walked across the parade ground to the Chester Beatty Library where Kitty showed him some of the Chinese and Asian woodcuts and scrolls as if they were her possessions. John-Joe took as great a delight in her pride as he did in the undoubted beauty of what she was showing him.

As they moved down Dame Street an enormous poster caught his eye. It was for the *Danann* and Kitty was right, the graphics were very powerful and appealing. A giant, muscular figure stretched across the full width of the poster, his hurley poised over his shoulder for a swing, his head and stick bursting out of the frame, his eye on the ball that was suspended somehow above the poster and turned slowly. The *Danann* logo on his sleeve glittered and across the bottom of the poster, in the gold lettering which Kitty had described, was the slogan; "The world will be watching. Will you?"

"That's Vinnie?"

"Yes. Isn't he gorgeous? You'd run away with him."

The long day ended with a stroll along the Grand Canal as the sun, finally fulfilling its promise, gleamed on the still, mirror-like water. They stopped at a lock to watch a smart cruiser being let through. When they arrived, the paddles on the upper gate had been opened and the water was filling the lock chamber, the cruiser rising steadily to the level of upper pound. When the levels equalised, the lock-keeper leaned backwards on the massive balancing beam to ease the gate open and John-Joe and Kitty did the same on their side. With a friendly way and a thank-you, the man at the wheel guided the cruiser out of the lock and along the water towards the summit at Lowtown, County Kildare.

"Three days and he'll be on the Shannon," said Kitty.

"Nice."

"Yes."

By the time they got back to Oxmantown Road, they were both falling in love.

As Kitty unlocked the front door, John-Joe sang the chorus of the song they had heard in Grafton Street;

"One, two, three four, five, hunt the hare and turn her
Down the rocky road and all the way to Dublin
Whack fol lol de ra."

"If you wake Mammy she'll kill both of us. Come up. I want to show you something." She tiptoed up the stairs and John-Joe followed her up and into the room he was staying in. She made a bee line for the edit suite and, sitting on the chair, switched on all the equipment. Taking out one of the cards, she popped it into the editing machine and started to run it through at high speed.

"This is the only card I could find that had been used on the camera. He had it for about a month before he was killed."

She stopped the playback as a certain number showed on the counter window and beckoned to John-Joe who stopped examining the tiny camera and moved over to look at the screen.

He saw an old, roofless cottage in a rugged glen. Next to it and looming over it was a blasted old oak tree. It was a long shot and it slowly zoomed in on the cottage door.

"It looks like Kerry," said John-Joe.

"Yes," agreed Kitty. "And it's so familiar, though I can't identify it, even though I've looked at it time and time again. Each time, I feel I've almost recognised it and then… nothing."

"Was that shot on this camera?" he asked.

"Yes. Amazing quality. He had great ideas on how to use it. How he could make some really powerful stories for the station."

"What sort of stories?"

"With this camera, you can be very discreet. It can be hidden and operated from a distance. It has an enormous zoom and a great microphone so imagine the possibilities for an investigative reporter like Tomas."

"Kitty!" It was Mrs Ring, from her room.

"Coming, Mammy! She must have heard us. She'll want a nightcap. Back in a minute."

She left the room and John-Joe moved over to sit in front of the edit suite. The camera panned away from the cottage, tilted up and then slowly zoomed in on a distinctive rock at the top of the cliff. It was an impressive zoom.

"Well, I'd recognise that place if ever I saw it," mused John-Joe.

The shot ended and the screen filled with snow. John-Joe groped for the reverse button and hit it. The image on the screen started to reverse at high speed. He frantically pushed other buttons and the card stopped and started to play. On the screen came a close up of Kitty's face on a pillow. She looked as if she was sleeping. The camera panned along her body and John-Joe gasped. She was naked. The camera moved back up to her face. Her eyes were open and she was looking steadily at the camera.

John-Joe was sitting in shock when the door opened and Kitty came in. He turned and their eyes locked. She closed the door softly and walked over to him. Leaning past him, she stopped the playback. Her breast was on a level with his face. He moved his head forward and through the cloth he took her nipple gently in his mouth. It stiffened between his lips.

6

The reception area of the *Danann* was impressive. It was decorated in black, purple and gold and back-lit transparencies of the *Danann* team seemed to float a few inches away from the black walls. There was a black couch suspended, God knows how, above the floor and illuminated underneath. There was nothing else in the area except a golden globe in the centre of the room, hovering in midair. John-Joe approached it and a deep, sexy, female voice issued from it.

"Please state your name and whom you wish to see?" it cajoled.

"John-Joe Crosby. Here to see…"

For the life of him he couldn't remember O'Shea's first name, so he groped for the card in his pocket. A screen on the globe was suddenly filled with O'Shea's face.

"John-Joe, I'm delighted to see you here. Come up."

The screen went blank. The voice implored; "Will you please place your hand here?"

A hand-shaped panel was illuminated. John-Joe placed his hand on it.

"Look straight at the screen and speak your name and whom you are about to see."

"John-Joe Crosby," said John-Joe, stifling a giggle. "To see Pat O'Shea."

Immediately his face, an image of his hand and O'Shea's face appeared on the screen.

"Thank you, Mr Joe Crosby," the voice crooned. A card slid from the machine bearing his and O'Shea's photographs and the word 'Visitor'. "Please display this card while you are in the building. Take the lift to the fourth floor. Mr O'Shea will meet you at the lift door."

A panel in the wall behind the globe opened to reveal a lift. John-Joe fixed the card to his lapel with the clip provided and entered it. The doors whispered closed and the lift rose smoothly. After a few seconds, the door opened to reveal O'Shea, beaming and offering his hand.

"You won't regret this," he said as he pumped John-Joe's hand.

He ushered John-Joe along a hushed corporate corridor with *Danann* images on either wall.

"I'm only here to look."

"I understand your caution. No burning bridges until you've seen what's on the other shore."

They entered a magnificently-appointed office with a view over the city towards the Wicklow hills.

"And I'll tell you what's on the other shore for talent like yours. Excitement you haven't felt since you ran out into a decent stadium for your first inter-provincial match."

John-Joe went to the window and looked out.

"Playing with the big boys," continued O'Shea. "Playing for keeps. Playing better than you've ever played in your life before. Playing in a way that will make the whole world sit up and take notice. Sit down."

He gestured towards a deeply upholstered swivel chair facing the desk. John-Joe sat in it and couldn't resist pushing it in a circle. When he came through 360 degrees O'Shea's face was inches from his and he had a form and a pen in his hands.

"And more money that you've ever dreamed of. Sign this."

John-Joe took the form.

"A confidentiality agreement. Playing with the big boys?"

"Bigger than the boys your mother told you not to play with."

"Does this form have any value?

"It has the force of law behind it."

"And behind that?"

"Behind that is Jack Curran. And Jack Curran would make the devil himself hold his tongue. So total confidentiality, OK?"

"How total?"

"Not to labour the point..." O'Shea drew his finger across his lips and then across his throat. Then he spun the swivel chair – hard. He stopped it when John-Joe was facing the desk. John-Joe clicked the pen open and signed the form.

"Now," said O'Shea. "Let's have a look at what's coming to you."

The *Danann* gym was like the set of a science-fiction movie. It was cavernous, with exercise areas in pools of light stretching into perspective on all sides. Apart from the usual hi-tech exercise machines and implements – and there were plenty of those – there were strange contraptions and spaces, the purpose of which was hard to determine.

There were numerous Oriental men in white-linen costumes at work with people or leading them from place to place at a half run. Permeating the entire space was a soundtrack of male voices in wordless song, long, drawn-out vowel sounds, so deep as to be on the verges of human hearing. The sound was primal and disturbing and within seconds of being exposed to it, the ears resonated to the pitch and slow, inexorable rhythm of the music, if, indeed, it merited that appellation.

O'Shea led John-Joe over to the first lighted area. There were six men using what looked like ornamental versions of the new-style police batons.

“Tonfas,” explained O’Shea. “Thousands of years old. The cops have just discovered them.”

Under the guidance of a small-oriental man, the men were thrusting, swinging and punching in slow motion, each with two tonfas. They were all in perfect synchronisation except the man at the nearest end. The oriental moved up behind him and delivered a blow to his shoulder with the flat of his hand. A quickly-subdued wince was the only reaction and the man matched the next move, a figure-of-eight arc, impeccably.

At the next area, three men were practising with samurai swords, again under the guidance of an oriental instructor. In perfect formation they all held the swords in both hands, drew them back above their slightly-bent right legs, with their left legs stretched forwards. After a deliberate pause in that tensed position, they lunged forward, swords swishing through the air, with their weight transferred to their now-bent left legs. The forward movement was considerable and they held themselves almost motionless in that position, the sword tips far in advance of their bodies. The oriental moved in front of the outstretched swords and watched for any quiver. The swords were still. Reaching forward, he grasped each sword tip and pulled it forward another inch. The strain in each face was discernible.

O’Shea and John-Joe watched for another few minutes and then walked on.

“Now we’re getting into your territory,” he said.

He was right. Two men with hurleys were attacking the third man who had a wooden stick about two feet in length to defend himself. The blows were hard and he fended off most of them and shrugged off the rest.

Beyond them, a row of about eight men were moving in perfect synchronisation. Each held a hurley and was moving it in a rhythmic way around one forearm, under the armpit and across the back, around the other forearm, around the back of the neck and smack into the outstretched hand. A pause before twirling it the way Fred Astaire would have twirled a cane and then back into the routine. It was mesmeric and fascinating.

They moved further along, passing a man whose face was a mask of blood. He was being led away by one of the Orientals. John-Joe glanced at O'Shea who grinned.

"Big boys don't cry," he said.

Further along, one man with a hurley was standing in the middle of a large mat. Several men were throwing balls at him from the edge of the mat – fast and hard. He was spinning and ducking as he endeavoured to hit them all back to the thrower and he succeeded more times than not. There were other, more common fitness pursuits being carried out in the gym and at each of them John-Joe could sense the utter dedication in the relentless effort.

"Jack Curran has promised to have the best and the toughest hurling team the world has ever seen in Arena21 for the opening match," said O'Shea. "These men will be at the peak of fitness by then and the world will look at them in envy. Oh, and watch this."

They had reached another lighted area in which couples in black wide, swirling trousers and wearing grilled helmets were twirling and slashing at each other with what looked like bamboo canes. An oriental man in white was moving amongst them, watching each move closely. It took some minutes for him to realise that they were all women.

"Yes. Women," said O'Shea, who was watching his reactions all along. We haven't forgotten *camogie*. That will be launched later. And we have had no shortage of applicants. The girls start with kendo, some of the swordplay can easily be adapted to hurling. Just imagine the spectacle. We'd have to… update… the clothing of course, make it more sexy, like volleyball. Look what arse-splitting shorts did for that very boring sport. TV potential – that's the secret."

John-Joe said nothing. He was measuring his own state of

fitness against that of the men and women he had just seen and he knew he was seriously wanting. For the first time since he had played hurling competitively, he felt inadequate and it was a very uncomfortable feeling.

He parted with O'Shea in the foyer and made his way into the street. He was repelled and fascinated by what he had seen. He found it hard to believe that such tactics could be grafted onto the game of hurling as he knew it. Hurling was a game for raw-boned boys and men, to be played on makeshift pitches in all corners of Ireland, and on some well-maintained sports fields and, occasionally in a fancy stadium. There was a sort of homespun honour about it and he knew – he felt himself – that the men and boys and girls who played it were linked in some almost mystical way, with ancient Ireland. All the players felt a sense of strong Celtic identity as they kept alive the superb game. Would such crass and flashy antics destroy the very essence of the game? He wasn't sure. The current One Day Internationals in cricket got more TV time, even if didn't have the prestige, of Test Cricket. But there was room in the cricket world for both. Meantime he had felt excitement as he had watched the *Danann* preparations and he knew, deep down, that the excitement would communicate itself to the watchers and in the current age of extreme sport and almost reckless disregard for danger, the appeal would be widespread. He himself had enjoyed the occasional Far Eastern martial-arts movie and had tuned in on the various, highly sponsored, extreme sports events that stretched the human capacity for athleticism to the utmost. Men and women were achieving physical capabilities undreamed of decades ago. The old newsreels of earlier sporting events such as the first Olympics or even mid-twentieth-century team events looked cumbersome and awkward compared with modernday sportsmen and women and what they were achieving. There had been exceptions to the gradual improvements in the past hundred years, sportspeople who had stunned the sports world with giant steps in exceptional performances which emerged, it seemed, more from inherent physical abilities than from scientific training. Led by these and other giants, seconds and centimetres were being clipped off track and field events every year and superbly fit and dedicated teams in group sports were holding each other to goalless draws in highly paid and motivated team events all over the world. Today's power tennis – with serving speeds in excess of 250 kph regularly recorded – would have dismayed previous champions. This dimension, the wonderment of just how far a human mind and will could stretch the human body's capabilities were a major part of the attraction of sport. But nowadays such wonderment was almost exclusively limited to professional sport. To what heights could hurling, with its huge physical potential, rise if training to the extent he had just witnessed was applied? But that would necessitate professionalism and would professionalism ruin hurling? Not if one thought of Australian footie which was professional and occasioned the world's largest crowds of sports fans at the annual finals. Not if people like himself and Uncle Joe could make a comfortable living out of it, with possible enormous financial rewards while at the – short-lived – peak of their prowess and a decent salary from peripheral activities.

With such thoughts racing to and fro in his stimulated mind, he turned to look back at the *Danann* headquarters and the graceful bulk of the stadium. This was big time, big business and he knew, despite his reservations about the brutal tactics – in fact, perhaps because of them – he had to be a part of it. He had to pit his skills against the men that were being developed in the *Danann* gym. He had to find out if, hell, *prove*, that he was as good as their best and maybe even better.

He headed back to North Dublin with an excited glow in his stomach.

7

On the following Monday, John-Joe found his way into a ponderous six storey building overlooking one of the green squares in South Dublin. There he was escorted into a spacious but bare office in which a portly man sat behind an enormous, scruffy desk. On the desk was an incongruous grouping of a blotter, a well-handled intercom terminal, a computer terminal and a cut-glass ink stand and pen and pencil holder. The ink bottle, he noticed, was empty. The man reached forward and gestured towards one of the upright, armless and plastic-seated, wooden chairs facing the desk and kept his hand extended as John-Joe sat down. Seeing the hand still in mid-air, John-Joe rose again and grasped it. The man held it firmly but didn't shake it. He fixed John-Joe with a manly stare and smiled.

"John-Joe Crosby I presume?"

Seeing as how has had been announced by the man's secretary on the intercom and at the door as she opened it, John-Joe thought that it was a reasonable presumption.

"That's me," he said.

"That's you," the man concurred. "And I am Ignatius O'Leary, your… paterfamilias… for the foreseeable future. Sit down."

He released the hand and threw himself back into a light blue, cantilevered chair that shuddered under his considerable bulk and slid backwards from the impact. Pulling himself forward until his stomach grazed the desk, Mr O'Leary steepled his fingers and regarded John-Joe over them, again with the manly stare.

"You couldn't have come at a more opportune time. You being one of our foremost hurlers."

"Why is that?"

"Because, my fine friend, we are in the middle of processing a Commission of Enquiry into something that I'm sure will be of deep, personal interest to you."

He pressed the intercom button. "Miss Keogh, please bring in the Arena21 file."

John-Joe sat up a little straighter.

"Arena21?"

"I was right. I usually am. You *are* interested." The manly stare lasted until Miss Keogh came in carrying a slim file which she placed down in front of O'Leary. O'Leary waited until the door had close behind Miss Keogh.

"This," he intoned "will be on your desk in one hour." John-Joe rose halfway out of his chair but his forward movement was stopped by a raised hand and a slightly disapproving stare. "It will be brought to your office in due time and placed on your desk for your urgent attention. That is the process. A sound, honest and incorruptible process is what makes a bureaucracy great. Here, Mr Crosby, process is sacrosanct and that is why we have to keep growing our civil service, so that all such processes get proper, professional attention and action."

"Well, it will get so from me."

"I'm sure it will. That is why I deliberately held the process of this matter up until you joined us. Your intimate knowledge of the sport will be of enormous assistance and might even facilitate the process. We are always on the lookout for appropriate personnel for appropriate action."

"Do you always match employees to projects so exactly?" asked John-Joe, impressed in spite of himself.

"No. Very seldom. In fact, hardly ever." O'Leary swivelled his chair towards the window and gazed out. "You see, as the civil service grows, we have to hire more and more people and those people are of different levels of capabilities. Some good and appropriate, as you are, and some rather lacking in both ability and interest. So we keep hiring to keep all the necessary processes going without them suffering from unequal levels of competence. In fact, a civil servant is not necessarily required to understand the issue in hand, merely to facilitate the process. So your suitability is of rare benefit."

"I'm pleased. Is… er… the Commission of Enquiry report can't be in there. Can it?"

"Of course not."

"So… do I get to read it?"

"Of course not. It's not required."

"Then what's the point of me—"

"The process, Mr Crosby, the process. You will merely facilitate the process. The contents of the report are and will remain strictly confidential. If it were a Tribunal of Enquiry, it would be even more so but, and it saddens me to say it, an *Oireachtas* Enquiry, although it too should be completely confidential, is all too often bandied about by the politicians in the *Dail* until every Tom, Dick and Harry knows its intimate details as well as he knows the *Racing Report*."

"So you haven't read it?"

"No. It's not my business. The only Commission of Enquiry that I actually read was that on the apparition of the Blessed Virgin at Knock and that was when it was published on the internet in the 1980s. Now *that* was processed with consummate skill and perspicacity. Two commissions actually, one in 1879, shortly after the sightings happened and another in 1935 *and* it was only totally disseminated in 1979 when Pope John Paul XII himself bestowed a token of papal honour and recognition. I…" The stare grew steely. "Was part of that process."

"Any idea when *this* commission will have done its business?"

"None whatsoever. Curiosity on the part of a civil servant would be inappropriate." He pushed the file across the desk. "Miss Keogh will show you your office."

He pressed the intercom button and Miss Keogh opened the door and stood waiting in the doorway. A bemused John-Joe picked up the file and, nodding at O'Leary, made his way out of the office.

"Inappropriate, Mr Crosby."

That Wednesday evening John-Joe was playing in a practice match for Tim's club and they were well ahead. It was the last few minutes of the game and with the ball on his hurley, he nodded across the field at Tim, indicating where he should move. Once he was sure that Tim understood, he feinted to his left and stopping dead. The two opponents shot ahead of him, giving him enough space to feed Tim a low, fast pass. Tim was where he should be, he lengthened his already long stride and effortlessly, pucked the ball into the goal.

That goal ended the game and the teams shook hands with each other as they headed for the changing rooms. John-Joe and Tim walked side by side.

"It's great playing with you again," said Tim.

"Yes. It was good."

"A bit of a walkover for you, I'm afraid."

"Well played, John-Joe," said a teammate as they approached the building.

"Thanks," said John-Joe. "Yes. I'd like a bit more of a challenge."

"South Dublin Rangers next week. That won't be so easy."

"I suppose so."

"You don't sound so enthusiastic."

"I'm afraid I won't be playing next week."

"What!" Tim was aghast. "The team is relying on you."

"It's a good team. It'll do as well without me."

"In all the time I've known you, the only thing that would keep you away from a game was another game."

Tim stopped dead.

"You're going to the *Danann?*"

"Just to have a look. Joe asked me to."

"Your Uncle Joe?"

"He told me to find out about their methods. He thinks they'll kill the sport."

"And what do you think?"

"I don't know. I haven't made up my mind yet."

"Well, I think it will."

John-Joe stopped and moved towards the side of the field, away from the changing rooms. Tim followed. John-Joe spoke.

"How's the job?" he asked.

Tim looked taken aback at the seeming irrelevance.

"The job? The job is… the job."

"Do you enjoy it?"

"Well, not exactly."

"You hate it. Actually you don't even do that. You don't think about the job at all, when you're not doing… whatever the hell you do. Do you? What do you do anyway?"

"No. I don't. I'm… part of a process that evaluates the performance of the department."

"And how is the department performing?"

"What? OK, I suppose but why do you want to know?"

"I don't. Nor do you. Do you?"

"No. Not particularly."

"And what do you think you'll say to your kids when they ask you what you do at work? That you spend your time finding out something you actually didn't want to know? Because you

LEABHARLANN
CO. CILL DARA

didn't actually give a flying fuck. What will happen when you do 'evaluate the department?'"

"It's... it's an ongoing process. It sets a benchmark for efficiency... for..."

"Perpetual evaluation?"

"That's how a civil service works. Or should work—"

"Listen to yourself, Tim *a vic!* What you're doing has no value, no meaning and no sense for a hot-blooded Irishman who's among the best hurlers in Ireland. It's meaningless. It's a play-play job for a play-play problem."

Tim scratched his head ruefully.

"I suppose it is. It's just how things are."

"Well, it's how things shouldn't be. You should be doing something you care about. Something where you can apply the skills you're best at. Not pissing away your life doing nothing of value until you retire with a pension, a houseful of demanding kids and an ulcer as big as a *sliotar*. The trouble is, Tim, I'm going to be doing the same sort of thing if I'm not careful."

"So you've started at work?"

"No. I've started the start. I've spent the last three days starting to start my involvement in the process of starting a job."

"Oh, God. That sounds very familiar. That's how I felt when I started."

"Started what? The job, or the start of a job?"

Tim grinned ruefully. "I'm still not sure."

"And you never will be. Not until you reach the nose-bleeding heights of the SCSC—" He underlined the capital letters with his finger. "the Senior Civil Servant Clique. And by then your hurling days will be definitely over."

"So what are you going to do? Throw in the job – and the pension?"

"I don't give a fuck about the pension. I'll cruise along, pretending to be working until I sort out what really matters to me. And that means looking at Curran's lot."

"I suppose you're right. But is the *Danann* the way to go?"

"I don't know. But I'm going to find out. OK?"

Tim walked on silently.

"OK?"

"OK."

"I'll need your support, Tim. It'll be hard enough without losing a friendship I value above all. OK?"

"OK."

They turned towards the changing room, breaking into a trot and pulling in their shoulders to keep warm.

8

The next afternoon John-Joe pushed the glass door open and entered the reception of the graphic-design company where Kitty worked. The décor was retro industrial; concrete walls, exposed cast-iron I-beams and artfully-broken brick. The reception desk was composed of the sort of heavy-metal mesh of which factory cat- walks are made and the floor was covered in shiny-black rubber with raised, flat, circular protuberances. Metal-framed award certificates covered the walls. A painfully-shiny cast-iron bucket in the corner sported large paper tulips. The chairs were made of black metal with holes drilled all over them and the coffee table, composed of two old Mercedes radiator grills joined together by a slab of armour plate glass, had a fan of design magazines spread across it.

There was nobody in the room and John-Joe moved over to look at the awards. They were mostly American, with sparse, faint typography letter spaced to hell and gone and very stylish signatures in a range of ink colours. He was trying to make out the inscription on one of the awards when a young girl emerged from the back, making for the front door. She was dressed like a refugee from a charity shop, toting a butterfly emblazoned

Versage shopping bag and wearing an enormous pair of Mickey Mouse glasses.

"Howareye?" she said. "Are you looking for somebody?"

"Kitty Ring. I'm here to—"

"She's inside. KITTY!" she shrilled. "Someone to see you."

Then she was gone, closely followed by the Versage bag. John-Joe went into the back room. There were trestle tables around the periphery, each containing an Apple Mac, a stack of software packages and miscellaneous papers, proofs, colour charts and standard DTP tools and accoutrements. In the centre, a table contained several scanners and one or two laser printers. Next to it, on the floor, stood a large colour printer, the working end of which was crawling back and forth over an A1 size sheet of paper creating, line by line, a print of a *Danann* poster. *Danann* graphics were among the images pasted or pinned onto the white walls. Kitty was sitting in front of an Apple Mac at the back of the room.

"Hi Kitty. Are you ready?"

"Hi JJ. Won't be long. I'm sorting out some of Tomas's files."

John-Joe walked over and looked at the computer screen. There were three photographs displayed, one was of Curran, another of a model of Arena21 and the third of a man he didn't recognise. There was text next to each photograph. He leaned forward to read it.

"That's Doherty?" he asked.

"Yes, the minister in charge of public planning. And that's—"

"Curran. Yeah. I know. I've been busy on the internet, getting up to speed on the place."

"Why?"

"Because – you'll find this strange – I'm steering a Commission of Enquiry on Arena21 through the… processes at what's called work."

"And? Anything interesting?"

"Only what's out there."

"And the Commission?"

"That's not much use to man or beast. Kafka or Dostoevsky would be impressed. It's all so… Jesus!" he looked around the office. "This is a real job with real outcomes. What I do is… it's like shovelling wet oatmeal. It has no substance. I generate paperwork about other paperwork and I don't get to read the commission report because it's confidential, so I have no idea as to what the commissioners think, or know."

"It sounds like the usual cover-up. You'd be wasting your time trying to find out what happened." She gestured at the screen. "Tomas always did his own digging. And he was like a magpie."

Kitty scrolled down to reveal other items. "He'd collect things, rumours, hard information, pictures, cuttings, snippets from social media, whatever he could dig out, then he'd let a pattern emerge. He was at the magpie stage on this story."

A picture of a building came into view.

"That's the New Republic Bank. They were implicated in some sort of underhand dealings at the time the planning permission was granted."

"Any pattern?"

"Can't find one. It's all raw data. It was common knowledge that planning permission for the stadium was obtained far too easy, with too many key questions left unanswered, so his story obviously involved that."

"There was a lot of opposition, I believe."

"Not enough to make any difference. This doesn't lead anywhere. It's as if he moved to another story, because this was captured weeks before he died. He seems to have lost steam."

"Maybe he moved to another way of telling the story."

"Yes. The video. There must be another video card."

The printer gave a small 'ping' and Kitty got up to take the printout.

"I'll see if I can root anything out," said John-Joe.

"And where would you go rooting?'

"Arena21. I'm going there."

"How can you have anything to do with Curran?"

John-Joe indicated the graphics.

"How can you?"

"Ah, that's just work for their advertising agency. You'd be working directly with the bastard."

"I'm just going to have a look at their methods," John-Joe protested.

"You'll be working with the man that had Tomas killed."

"If that turns out to be true, I'll help you prove it."

She was unsure about that but she shut down her computer, locked the premises and let him take her for a meal and then to hear some music in a smoky pub. They both put Tomas and the *Danann* out of their minds and concentrated on being two healthy young people in love.

The meal, at a sushi bar, was not a success. The décor was that form of minimalism that sacrifices everything, even comfort, for style. The steel backrest on his chair caught his fourth vertebrae at its most uncomfortable and the stainless steel chopsticks were virtually unmanageable. Kitty loved sushi but John-Joe found the taste of raw fish decidedly unpleasant and the warm sake revolting. He was dying for a good steak, medium, with thick gravy over golden roast potatoes – and a pint. When he shared this vision with Kitty, she went into a long diatribe about the inherent conservatism of the Irish and how unprepared they were for the modern world. John-Joe listened with equanimity, she looked stunning with her eyes flashing and besides, it took his mind off his discomfort and the sushi. Later in the evening the music was good. The group played rock music with a traditional Irish base, so it appealed to them both. They played a rocking version of *Sean O'Dwyer of the Glen,* featuring a solid, heavy-handed bass player, which had them both finger bopping. Kitty looked good and knew it and the pint was cool and smooth. However, when they got back to Oxmantown Road, she wouldn't go into his room, even though Mrs Ring's gentle snoring was audible and Tim was out somewhere.

John-Joe lay awake for a long time, his mind churning with visions of Kitty's lovely body and how enthusiastically she had used it to pleasure him the other night and how clinging she was tonight. Images from the Tomas' video kept intruding too, he was disturbed and excited about what he had seen on it. Then again, he had to face a major decision regarding his job.

For the first time in his healthy life, he had doubts about his physical toughness. The exercises he had seen at the gym were the most strenuous he had ever seen. To play hurling with men so well trained would call for more than his skill and agility. It would call for a toughness and ruthlessness that had never been asked of him.

Was he really up to it? He dropped off to sleep in a state of doubt.

9

John-Joe was wearing the *Danann* training outfit and feeling very comfortable with the thin, flexible and skin-tight material with leather reinforcing around the shoulders, elbows and knees. A thin metal box protected his genitals and he wore a light leather helmet and baseball boots with particularly anti-slip soles. The half-gloves he wore protected the knuckles and back of the hand but left the fingers free. He was a devotee of the traditional *caman* and a fastidious chooser of his own hurleys, so he was slightly offended when O'Shea thrust into his hands what was obviously a synthetic stick. He had studied the making of the traditional hurley by spending one entire school summer holiday working at hurley-making factory and had followed the process from forest to the playing field. He had assisted one of the foresters in the ash forest near his home. It was in a small, sparse plantation on what the forester told him was free draining, nutrient rich soil in a frost-free part of the county. He had helped trim away the ground vegetation around likely trees and watched as they felled a suitable ash with a proper base and regular toes which were the upper parts of the roots. The outward curving of these were essential because the curving grain in the sapwood would be sculpted so that it curved out into the *bas* (the base) of the hurley, imbuing it with the natural strength of the tree – the strength that supported the tree would support the *bas* under the extreme pressure of the sport. The manufacturing process was fascinating, each stick trimmed roughly with a band saw which produced inch-wide hurley shapes of the clean, living sapwood with the curving grain, avoiding the inert heartwood which was too brittle. These were then properly shaped by a silent old man with a deftly-wielded sander and a well-used spoke shave, so sharp it seemed to sing as it moved through the wood. Under this man's skilful administrations, the long, evenly-spaced grain glistened as it fulfilled all its potential in the finished stick. It was the way a real hurley had been made for centuries and a synthetic stick seemed a sacrilege. However he took the jet black hurley, felt the superbly balanced heft and flexed it against the ground. It had the required balance of resilience and resistance and he had to admire the rays of dark purple reflections that ran up and down it as it bent and straightened.

"There's hemp in there. A cannabis plant. Better than glass fibre in reinforced plastics because it's strong. Mercedes use it in their cars, for Christ's sake. It has greater insulation, so your hands don't sweat so much and it has extra flexibility in movement, so it has greater whip when you use it. And if you lose a match, you can smoke the fucking thing," O'Shea explained. "It's time ash moved over and anyway, they can't grow enough of the right-quality trees fast enough. This is the latest in chemistry. It's mixed and moulded under extreme tension and has an uncanny memory. Hit the ball cleanly and it will go through a wall."

"Or a man," said John-Joe.

O'Shea shrugged. "Come on, we'll get you measured."

"For what?"

"The specs for your own special hurley."

They were in the *Danann* gym and the disturbing voice track was still playing softly. O'Shea ushered John-Joe into a booth which contained a ring of cameras around the perimeter of a circular mat. He was placed in the centre of the mat and another oriental – they were everywhere! – started to attach Velcro mounted electrodes to various parts of his body, checking their appearance as pinpoints of light against a glowing graph on a computer screen which was facing them. John-Joe moved his free arm which had an electrode attached to the back of his hand, his wrist, forearm, elbow and front and back of his shoulder. The pinpoints of lights moved accordingly, leaving smooth tracks behind them. When his whole body had been covered, O'Shea handed him the black hurley. He swung it around his body and was amused to see its path traced on the screen while counters whirred. The technician moved to sit in front of the screen and turned it to face him. He glanced at O'Shea.

"Right," said O'Shea. "We want you to go through your entire repertoire of movements when you're playing. Make it fast and don't be afraid to repeat the movement if it doesn't feel right."

"My entire repertoire?"

"We have something to prompt you. Look."

On another screen, facing the mat, a high-angle video recording of John-Joe in action in the Fifteen Acres appeared. The camera was on him at all times as he played. He gasped and looked at O'Shea.

"What the—"

"We've had our eye on you for a while. Now follow the movements."

John-Joe shrugged and did what he was told, improvising a little as he went and putting some grace notes into his play, where he thought his move should have been smoother or better balanced. He got into the swing of things and began to enjoy himself, basking a little in appreciation of his own undoubted grace and obvious strength. When the exercise was finished, attention turned to his dominant hand. He slipped on a snug-fitting metallic glove and grasped the hurley and a slioter. He tapped the ball up and down, gently and harder and waved the hurley all around in all possible positions. O'Shea, stepped on to the mat and grasped the far end of the hurley and bade John-Joe resist him as he pulled, twisted and agitated the hurley. After sometime, they stopped the operation and John-Joe nodded at the inscrutable oriental who was frantically tapping the keyboard.

"Now all that data will be fed into the moulding manufacturing unit and a hurley produced, minutely designed to match the physical and muscular demands you place on your body and, of course, on the hurley. It will be perfectly balanced in use. It has a better memory than wood ever could, it will spring instantly back into the desired configuration, no matter what strain you put on it in play. And, if anything should happen to it – unsustainable stress or shock – another identical one can be produced in minutes. In the meantime, use that hurley."

O'Shea indicated another Oriental man who was beckoning John-Joe to approach him where he stood on a large mat with goalposts at one side. He threw the ball at John-Joe as the latter stepped onto the mat. Then he gestured at the goal, at the same time, indicating several men with hurleys to form a line between the goal and John-Joe. They did so, each a hurley's length from the other. Crouched, they awaited John-Joe's attempt on goal.

John-Joe fingered the ball. It was the same size and configuration as a normal ball excepting that the raised seams were much harder and it sat heavier in the hand, it had the sort of dead weight that indicated an extremely dense and heavy core, perhaps lead or some such heavy metal. He tossed it in the air and caught it on his hurley, tapping lightly. He was surprised by how high up in the air it went with such a light tap. Adjusting his whole body and muscle tension to the synergy between ball and stick, he slashed it as hard as he could directly at the centre of the line of men knowing what their reactions would be. Instinctively, the men in the centre moved towards the point of impact, leaving a gap on each side large enough for John-Joe to penetrate, keeping his elbows close to his side. He was through before they knew it and he had time to reach across and scoop the ball from the stick of the man who had stopped it. John-Joe turned on his heel and prepared to hit the ball into the goal but his satisfaction at having beaten five men was banished by a blow to his hurley so ferocious that his shoulder went numb with pain and he stopped dead in his tracks.

It was Vinnie.

"That's not good enough for the *Danann*," Vinnie gloated as he turned towards the other men. John-Joe was led by the inscrutable trainer to the next grouping of learners and teachers. The line of men had their feet clamped to the ground and their arms were bound behind their backs. John-Joe's trainer indicated the men and tossed a ball at him. It was clear what had to be done. Relying totally on his anti-slip soles, John-Joe ran towards the left side of the first man, slashed the ball across behind his back and, changing direction, he caught it on his hurley on the man's right side. This feint confused the second man sufficiently for John-Joe to dash through to the far side but the third man was ready for him. His shoulder caught John-Joe as he dashed through the gap and almost knocked him to the ground. He recovered his balance but stayed crouched as if stunned and his deception was enough to fool the next man into relaxing his tensed body a fraction. John-Joe flicked the ball into the air and hurled himself at the man's chest. The man collapsed and John-Joe was past and already coiled for the rebound as the ball came back onto his hurley. He drove the ball straight at the next man's face and the man ducked his head, catching the ball on his leather helmet. The force of the blow, however, drove all thoughts of stopping John-Joe in his next charge from the man's mind. John-Joe was through.

The next contest involved a narrow beam, two metres above the ground with steps up to each end. John-Joe climbed up onto the beam at the trainer's silent instructions and turned to face the person who mounted the far end of the beam. It was Vinnie. The objective was clear and they approached each other carefully, hurleys extended. Several thrusts and parries were exchanged as each tried to ascertain the other's balance. Then several swipes and lunges brought them closer to each other. Suddenly they both lunged at precisely the same moment and clashed, with crossed sticks within an arm's length. Their strengths were almost equally matched as they pushed hard. A slight lessening of the pressure persuaded John-Joe to draw back his stick for a blow. It was a mistake. The handle of Vinnie's hurley was suddenly buried in his stomach just below the ribs. The pain negated his sense of balance and he fell to the floor, rolling to one side to absorb the force of the landing a little. Without a moment's hesitation, Vinnie launched himself at John-Joe, his feet aimed at his chest. Somehow, John-Joe found extra energy and momentum to continue the roll and Vinnie's feet connected with his shoulder as he rolled away. The fall stunned them both momentarily.

After several more sessions that taxed him to the limit of his strength and reflexes, John was placed, by the totally unsympathetic trainer on a treadmill. Since the speed of the machine was not too fast, John-Joe settled into an easy pace and emptied his mind as the rhythm took over. He was brought back to full alertness by a dramatic increase of speed. Instead of the pitiless trainer, it was Curran who stood by the controls. He watched as John-Joe got his balance and rhythm back again and then slowed the speed down considerably. John-Joe was expecting something of the sort and adjusted easily.

"The ancient disciplines of the East and the indomitable

courage and tenacity of the ancient Celt," said Curran, increasing the speed almost to maximum. "Two cultures. Both built on the glory of man in his natural state – that of combat. One culture lost in the mists of time and the darkness of legend. The other nurtured until recently behind a barrier of oriental inscrutability that kept the modern, thin-blooded world at bay."

Curran slowed the machine to a stop and John-Joe stepped off. Curran led him over to the benches and gestured for him to lie on one. As he spoke, he loaded several weights onto the bars that rested above John-Joe's chest.

"Imagine," he said, lifting the plates with ease, "the headlong, exuberant excess of the ancient Gael and the heroic stillness and poise of the Samurai."

The weights were to his satisfaction. He nodded John-Joe to begin pressing.

"The Samurai principles of *bushido*, the way of the warrior, have been kept alive in the gyms of the world but until I came along, nobody thought of resuscitating the fighting spirit of the Gael. It's been forgotten, ignored, even laughed at," he snorted. "Even the mediaeval stick fighting of the Irish has been reduced to a music-hall image. The shillelagh! What is it now but the comic prop of a bog trotter."

Curran stopped John-Joe and guided the bars back onto their rest. He added another plate onto each end and gestured him to start pressing again. John-Joe could get the weights up, but only just. Curran kept on talking.

"The *Danann*. The *Thuathe de Dana*. The people of Dana. A name, a concept to conjure with. What Irishman can hear that name without being transported back to the days of glory in Ireland. I have recreated that image, that reality, in a body of men honed to an incredible degree of fitness. Hold it there!"

John-Joe had his arms at full stretch. He held the bar aloft, arms quivering.

"That is your peak," said Curran, crouching next to John-

Joe. "Hold it. Visualise your muscles here, and here, filling with nutrient-rich blood. Hold that peak. Longer. Longer."

The intensity of his whisper inspired John-Joe to hold the bar up until he thought the muscles and sinews of his arms would explode. To his surprise, he managed to sustain the effort for several seconds before he let the bar drop onto the rests.

"Good. You are in excellent physical condition but my men have had a long start over you. They all came here after training by their betters. Men who passed on the same methods they had used in their successful days. So their methods were – and are – a generation out of date. We start afresh. We take them into areas they never dreamed of, areas where the achievement rates are measured by methods they only understand when they see the result in more performance than they thought possible."

He produced a card and handed it to John-Joe. "This man will help you catch up." Curran rose and made a drinking motion at one of the trainers who scurried away.

"Imagine," continued Curran, "if you had refused to walk upright when mankind stopped swinging in the trees and strode over the limitless savannas."

O'Shea arrived with a cup of bright-yellow liquid. Curran took the cup and handed it to John-Joe.

"Sip that slowly," he said. "Don't worry. It's legal. How far do think I could take these men if there was any suspicion of doping? Right now, your glycogen needs replenishing after that effort." He stood up and picked up his train of thought. "Imagine if you had refused to use the first stirrup, draw the first bow or pull the first trigger. Imagine what you would have missed. Soon, in stadiums, on television, on the internet, millions will experience the explosive power of hurling at the best, combined with the focus and dedication of the martial arts of the east." He walked away. O'Shea drew some papers and a pen from his jacket pocket.

"One contract. One pen," he said, offering them to John-Joe.

"And one million Euros."

Curran turned and called back to him.

"Join me, Mr Crosby," he said. "And make the game great."

John-Joe signed.

10

The steps leading down to the basement smelt of urine and sweat. Through the dirt-encrusted windows he could see large shapes lumbering about and could hear the sound of grunts and heavy bodies on a complaining wooden floor. He approached the door and tried the handle. It opened and he moved through into a dim, decrepit gym. The lumbering shapes were men who carried the equivalent of John-Joe's total weight in sheer muscle about their chests and massive arms and legs. They were using dumbbells, squatting, pressing weights and punching gargantuan bags with a ferocious and intense concentration. Hamstrings, biceps, triceps, thighs, calves and abdomens bulged, rippled, popped, strained and swelled all around and such an amplitude of powered flesh made John-Joe feel decidedly undersize. He made his way through the sweat impregnated air and the slowly exercising men to the glass-fronted office at the back of the gym.

Seated at a desk in the office was the largest man John-Joe had ever seen. He was wearing a sleeveless vest and the countless muscles and sinews in his exposed body seemed all to have an independent life of their own. Their contractions and expansions seemed to have no bearing on what his limbs were doing. He reached for the telephone and an entire continent of subcutaneous explosions occurred along his massive arm. Even his ear appeared to grab the earpiece in a stranglehold. John-Joe knocked on the glass of the open door and walked in. The man looked up.

"Mr O'Connor?" asked John-Joe.

"Call me Bull."

"OK Bull, I'm John-Joe Crosby."

"Speak later," he said and hung up. He reached into a drawer and extracted a rosary. The movement sent his deltoid undulating.

"Curran has been on. There's a lot to be done to you," Bull's voice had lumps in it, like his body. He noticed John-Joe's glance at the beads.

"Relax. I use them as worry beads." As the beads moved through his fingers, the tendons and muscles in his hands flexed and played under the skin. At the same time, the desk behind which Bull was sitting was rocking from side to side, lifted by Bull's thighs rising and falling alternately. Bull's other hand was squeezing and releasing a tough rubber ball in the other hand. The rhythmic play of muscles across Bull's upper body was mesmerising. Suddenly Bull's ugly, creased face broke into a wide grin and that set off another radial motion, right up into his scalp.

"I've got to keep it in shape."

"I suppose so."

"No. What I mean is, if I let all this shit go soft, I'll look like a sack of manure. Can't make *you* look like this, though."

"I wouldn't want to..."

"Don't blame you. I haven't looked in a mirror for years. It looks bad enough from here."

He flexed his arm and looked down.

"Will you look at that," he said, meaning his biceps and triceps which sprang several inches into the air. "It's like two pythons wanking each other. No wonder she wouldn't go out with me."

"Who?"

"The mot I did all this for. I put on all this muscle so's she'd look at me. Turned out she likes them thin and interesting. The way I was before I started this shit. Now I'm trapped in it all. Mots!"

"Look, I'm joining the *Danann* and—"

"You have a lot of catching up to do. I worked on them and gave them their regime about a year ago and you've only got a month to the big match."

"They're a tough lot."

"It's not just the toughness, it's staying tough and keeping your energy up for ninety minutes. You're a mesomorph. That means—"

"I know what it means."

"Yeah. You'll never get really big. No big muscles either but I can help you increase your bulk, anabolics and stuff if you want."

"No thanks."

"You're right. And doping?"

He watched the shocked expression on John-Joe's face. "Relax. How long do you think I'd last if I encouraged that? They're even trying gene doping now. So you can create an athlete in the fucking womb. How about that? Out pops generation after generation of super fucking humanoids, impossible to test. Are you fast?"

"Very."

"Well then we'll concentrate on the cardiovascular, building an aerobic base. Then the muscles, calisthenics there. Finally, flexibility, a permanent stretch in your muscles and connective tissues to give you full joint range of movement. OK?"

"OK."

"Then the right amount of starch, iron and potassium. As a Kerryman, you'll be glad to know it'll be mostly from potatoes.

You'll load every third day, then every fourth day then every third day. Also steak. As bloody as you can manage. And supplements I'll give you. Got that?"

"Got it."

"OK. You do what I say and do those mad fucking exercises that Curran has those chinks teaching and you'll be as good as the rest. Better, if you start out as a really good hurler. Are you a really good hurler?"

"Yes."

"OK. Let's get started."

He hauled himself to his feet and left the office. John-Joe followed, trying to stop watching the protuberances on Bull's back, the motion of which was making him queasy.

Later that day, John-Joe bought a notepad and some envelopes and, sitting in a coffee house, wrote a short letter of resignation addressed to O'Leary. It was goodbye to the civil service forever. The service had a long memory, so he'd never get back in and he'd lose his pension but the money O'Shea was dangling in front of him made the pension almost laughable. Would he miss the Service? No. And the processes certainly wouldn't miss him. When he posted the letter he felt a weight slip off his shoulders. A weight he hadn't known he was carrying until it disappeared. Now he could concentrate on a hurling (Curran-style) life in a Dublin he was enjoying.

And there was Kitty.

John-Joe settled into the training routines, with Bull's diet and the *Danann* gym and the results were gratifying. Before the week was out, he had gone through as much detox as his strong, well-cared for body required. His musculature was well defined but not obtrusive and his skin tone was pink and glowing. He felt an extra spring in his step and a readiness to leap out of bed in the morning. Also his capabilities in bed with Kitty, when she agreed to be intimate again surprised and gratified him, although, to his slight chagrin, she seemed to take it for granted.

His confidence at the *Danann* gym grew swiftly and he lost his fear of the other players but never his respect. Vinnie left him alone, even though the mutual dislike was palpable whenever they were in close proximity to each other. Curran seemed pleased with his progress and he soon found his level amongst the top players there.

He soon discovered that, while he had a good chance of becoming the physical equal of the best of them, he lacked their viciousness and ruthlessness. They seemed to take a grim satisfaction in hurting each other and would summon hidden depths of energy just to inflict pain. Part of him understood this as a weakness in the sort of sport that was being developed but he felt he could keep up without seeking and exploiting the reservoir of hate that they all seemed to possess. But he knew that he was playing hurling better than he had ever played it before and better than he thought it possible to play. He wondered if the rest of Ireland team had any idea of the forces that were going to be unleashed on them. Curran soon enlightened him at one of his regular pep-talks.

"Just so's you don't get over confident," he said to the assembled players. "Let it be understood that I have informed Duggan of most of our techniques and offered him our hurleys."

There was a gasp of disbelief.

"Did you think I was going to offer you an easy victory? What would be the point of that? This new-style sport must be experienced, from the first match, as something revolutionary. People must understand from the outset that this is the future of professional sport. That they can expect every player to give his all, even at the risk of split heads and broken bones. This is sport that has never been seen in the safe, secure stadiums of the developed world. This is a primal struggle, known to many so-called primitive tribes but forgotten by the thin-blooded societies of today."

He paused to let that sink in.

"However, just because they have been informed of our techniques, they mustn't think they know all our tricks, must they?"

He smiled at the raucous laughter from the relieved players. Everybody seemed happy, except John-Joe and the row of inscrutable Orientals at the back of the auditorium.

That night John-Joe stood inside his bedroom and surveyed it. Good and all as the digs were, it was still only a room and his possessions were sparse to say the least of it. All he had was what he had brought to Dublin in a suitcase. His only expense was the modest rent he paid Mrs Ring and the occasional date he had with Kitty. She, in any case, was now working overtime most nights and weekends on the *Danann* account and both of them were usually pretty tired after a busy day and the generous suppers Mrs Ring supplied. But not tonight. Tonight he was fired up, as if he had surplus energy, generated by the day's training and motivational lectures which, in spite of his scepticism, stirred him up and planted an expectation in his bones and muscles that seemed partly sexual, it was so exciting. He tore off his jacket and changed into shorts, sports shirt and running shoes and, putting the front door key into a pocket in the shorts, slipped down the stairs and out into Oxmantown Road.

The night was cold, clear and lit by a three-quarter moon high in the heavens. Turning south he started to run down the middle of the road which, approaching midnight, carried very little traffic. Down through the narrow streets past the stately grey prison at Arbour Hill with its attendant church and cemetery containing the remains of the executed Easter Rising participants and the looming, glooming Collins barracks – now a museum – and onto the Quays. Turning towards the city centre he pounded along the pavement overlooking the dark greasy Liffey and seemed to be the last person alive in Dublin. He felt tireless, his shoes comfortable, all his orifices tight, his balls felt like *sliotars*, all his muscles functioning smoothly, his breath coming and going, ten long strides to each in-and-out breath, his heart ever so slightly above its normal, resting speed, his senses heightened and his feeling of power invincible. So when he heard the sound of raucous, drunken shouting and laughing ahead, he felt no qualms about his safety. He saw them ahead, about ten of them, reeling and staggering towards him down the middle of the road, loaded with drink and bursting with animosity towards anything or anyone who wasn't as pissed as they were. One of the throng, slightly more sober than the rest saw him and shouted with delight.

"Look boys. A fucking athlete. In the middle of the fucking night. Who the fuck does he think he fucking is?"

"The fucker! Let's get him!"

The rest of them shouted in gleeful agreement and, spreading out, across the pavement and into the road they moved in a rough semi-circle towards John-Joe, staggering less than before and quieting into a feral silence as he approached without slackening his pace.

"The fucker thinks he'll get past us."

"Into the Liffey with the fucker."

"Let's see if he can swim a good as he can run."

It was all going to be so easy. He could sense their inebriation, their slack bellies, their wheezy chests, their limp muscles and clumsy slowness as he came closer and closer. They seemed to be moving at a tenth of his speed and seemed to be pressed to the ground under a much greater force of gravity then he was. He kept up his speed and his direction – straight at them. He swerved past the first two and ducked under the outstretched arms of three more and to his disappointment, was suddenly on the far side of the group. Too easy. He turned back and ran through the group again, again dodging the disjointed arms that reached towards him. They started to howl with rage and frustration and moved in on him. But he wasn't there. A side slip took him to another part of what was now a seething mob of staggering bodies. One was bent over away from him, offering a saggy arse. Obligingly he kicked it, making sure that the soft front of his shoe slipped between the legs and his instep connected with the genitals.

Then he turned away and resumed his run. The kicked man regained his breath and screamed and several of his mates started in pursuit, shouting their limited stock of obscenities. He kept his pace down so that some of them began to gain on him but by their laboured breathing he could judge just where they were. When only one of them seemed to be within reach, he stopped and turned, hand on hips and still breathing normally. The fellow stopped, glanced quickly behind and saw that he was alone with this calm, crazy, running fucker. John-Joe stared into his eyes for a moment, enjoyed the sudden change from rage to fear and then turned and loped towards O'Connell Bridge.

Behind him the screaming and cursing started again but with far-less vehemence. The long way back, he decided, right through the north side of the city. Settling down into a steady pace, he let his body do the work and his mind do the wandering, all on the glories of sport and the truly great sports people. Christy Ring who had dominated his game and his childhood with his never-ending hurling victories and awards. Henry Shefflin who was the most decorated hurler in the world. Ever. Jesse Owens, who had run German pride into the ground at the 1936 Olympics and had Hitler's moustache bristling with rage. Fanny Blankers-Koen who used to have his father roaring with delight as 'The Flying Housewife', on her days off from minding her two kids, won eight events at the 1948 Olympics. Emil Zátopek, the 'Czech Locomotive' and the long-distance marvel who ran ten kilometres every morning with his wife on his back, clutching a stopwatch. Harrison Dillard, the one-hundred-metres world champion that his father travelled in the 1950s to see in Dublin at Dalymount Stadium (forbidden to GAA sportspeople). 'Jaysus! You should have seen him, black as the ace of spades, sure Dublin didn't know what to make of him, sparkling in red, white and blue, making all the rest look half starved. The Fastest Man in the World, he was then and he looked it too as he ran the distance before the other eejits got off the starting blocks. "Open the gates," the crowd shouted because they were too near the end of the track and it looked as if he'd run right through them. I never saw anything like it, before or since.' When he at last turned into Oxmantown Road, he broke into a sprint and, as fast as he could, covered the length of the road in seconds. This was the sort of explosive, all out bodily strain which took his heart and lungs to their limits. It could not be sustained but, as long as it lasted, it brought his entire physique to a pitch that made him feel he was supernatural. At the door, he doubled over and waited until his body resumed its natural rhythm.

It was good to be alive, and be John-Joe Crosby, master of the Dublin night and on the verge of great adventure in a sport he loved.

11

Tim was drunk and morose.

"It was humiliating."

"Ah. It's only a game," said Mrs Ring as she poured from the dwindling bottle of poteen.

"I never thought I'd live to see a member of the Ring family say that."

"That's because you only talk to the men. Anyway, being beaten is part of the game."

"We'd have run rings around them if John-Joe had have been there. But, it's not only that. He's playing around with Curran. Helping to kill the game."

"It'll take a lot to kill a game that's driven Irishmen mad since… forever."

Tim stared at the embers, grunting quietly to himself. They both straightened at the sound of the front door opening. Footsteps moved down the hall and the door opened to reveal John-Joe. He came in.

"Evening."

"Evening, John-Joe," said Mrs Ring, indicating a chair for him to sit on. John-Joe took a seat, looking at Tim, who was glaring at him. He waited, knowing that Tim would say what was on his mind.

"You realise," said Tim, through clenched teeth. "That we're out of the county competition now. Thanks to you and the bloody *Danann*."

"You know as well as I do that a team that has to rely on one man to win doesn't deserve to win."

"We would have won if you hadn't come and spoiled our rhythm."

"I only played with you twice."

"We all expected you to stay."

"I never said I would. We never discussed any commitment."

"I'm sorry I brought you in the first place," Tim got to his feet unsteadily. "I was so... I'm going to bed. I can't stand to look at you."

He made a dignified exit, erect and stiff. John-Joe sighed and looked at the embers. Mrs Ring finished her drink.

"Don't mind what he says. Ever since he heard you were coming to Dublin, he hasn't stopped talking about you. He says you'll become another Christy."

"He was part of your family, wasn't he?"

"Every Ring family in Ireland claimed Christy. But he was my uncle once removed," she paused and looked closely at him. "Do you know what you're getting into, son?"

"I'm not sure."

"Will that man ruin the game?"

"He'll either ruin it or..."

"Or what?"

"Turn it into the greatest game in the world."

"Some – like Tim – would say it's already that."

"I mean recognised as the greatest – worldwide."

"And I suppose the most profitable."

"Maybe that too. And where's the harm in that?"

"Not much harm. Profit hasn't destroyed soccer, has it?"

"No. It hasn't. You know Mrs Ring, I'd love to answer 'I'm a professional hurler' when anybody asked me what I did for a living."

"That'd have a nice ring to it, wouldn't it?"

"It would Mrs Ring."

She offered the bottle.

"Have a drop."

"No thanks. I'm in strict training now."

"You're with Curran?"

"For the moment, yes."

"I think you're doing the right thing."

"Well, that's good to know. I would have thought that you, of all people—"

"Of all people, among the most put upon. By three generations of men who dedicated their lives to hurling, to the exclusion of all else. Never a steady job, except for those with some sort of other skills, like making the hurleys, or tending the ash forests and even then, they couldn't get on. Hadn't the knowledge or the skills that those jobs needed to make them a career. Career! A few years at the top, where they'd get some money and trophies they could hock and then? Nothing. Nothing you could earn a living at. Not even a pension, only the state pension and God knows that's not much. Look at your uncle. A few years of glory and praise from all around and then only the training and the market garden he's trying to run. Nothing put by. But you now, John-Joe. You've got your head screwed on right."

"I've resigned the ould job."

"How did you feel when you did?"

"Free… somehow."

"That means you did the right thing."

"You think so?"

"I know so. Look at Kitty. She's moved on. Into a world I can't even get my head around. There's nobody in the whole of Kerry that would understand what she does. After generations of doing the same things again and again. The same jobs. Again and again. The same boring, hard lives, there's some of us who are going forward and taking a chance on the new ways that are upon us. Good luck to them all. And good luck to you John-Joe Crosby."

She tipped the bottle into her glass and shook it.

"Only a little left. There must have been a hole in the bottle. And go easy on Tim."

John-Joe nodded and rose to his feet. Then he stooped and kissed Mrs Ring on her forehead.

"Will you get out of that! Save them for Kitty."

He laughed and left the room. Mrs Ring looked into the embers and smiled.

"A professional hurler."

The next morning found Uncle Joe in Dublin for a meeting of the GAA and to see 'how his nephew was coming along' but John-Joe understood that he was there to find out what was happening as regards the *Danann* and set out to reassure him as best he could that he was investigating the situation from the inside before committing himself. The two of them had sat in the front room of the seedy North Dublin hotel that Joe had insisted on staying at, because his family and colleagues had always stayed there. The room was over furnished with upholstered and sofas and easy chairs and dim, pockmarked mirrors and dim portraits hung on every wall. It smelled of damp, disinfectant and disappointment and John-Joe couldn't wait to get out. He persuaded his uncle to come to Mulligan's for a couple of their renowned pints and he felt sure it would remind him of the pubs in Kerry.

"It's like no other sport you've ever seen, Uncle Joe. It's brutal, dangerous and... very exciting. And the training! I can do tricks with a hurley that would—"

"Tricks is it? I've never played a trick with my caman in my life. It's skill, my boyo."

"Skill then. I'm more skilled now that I ever was."

"Are you telling me you've learned more in the past month than I've taught you since your arse was the size of a shirt button?"

John-Joe extricated his foot.

"It's just a different approach, Uncle Joe. The game's still the same."

"The same! I hear there's no referee in the new rules. What's that mean?"

"There's a panel of adjudicators."

"Adjudicators my arse! You need a man on the ground, watching, understanding the mood of the game – or the man."

"I think that the new game will attract thousands – millions of spectators."

"Millions! Where's the stadium big enough for millions, for Christ's sake?"

"You don't understand. There's the stadium, sure, but there's also world-wide television and the internet. The world will want to see hurling. Nothing beats actually being there at the match but the real money comes from broadcasting."

"Aah. So it's all to do with money?"

"Yes. No. Money to develop the game, train new people to play—"

"It's disgusting. That's what it is. And I want nothing to do with it. And you should have nothing to do with it either, do you hear me, now?"

"Just imagine, Uncle Joe, if the whole world was interested in hurling, not just less than half of Ireland? What would that do to the game?"

"Destroy it."

"No, Uncle Joe."

"Destroy it. Other countries playing hurling? Bollocks! I want no Patafuckin'gonians playing the game Setanta played. Bigob, you're no flesh of mine."

"Aaah. You say that every time I miss a goal."

"Well, this time I mean it," Crosby was hurt. "I'm away back to Kerry."

"Stay. I'll show you a bit of Dublin."

"I've seen enough of Dublin."

But of course, he hadn't. He wanted to see Croke Park again, the scene of his many triumphs. He wanted to visit Kilmainham Gaol, where the 1916 rebels were executed. He wanted to look at Micheál Mac Liammóir's grave on the Hill of Howth and he wanted to walk around St. Patrick's Cathedral where Dean Swift created Gulliver and the Yahoos. He took a leaflet and flicked through it as they left the Cathedral.

"Bigob. He was a Protestant."

"Swift?"

"Yeah," a philosophical shrug. "Ah well. I won't hold that against him."

"I'm relieved."

His was an alternative tour of Dublin and John-Joe found it stimulating and thought provoking. They didn't refer to the *Danann* again, even though they both knew that the topic was simmering in each other's mind and even though the posters for the match were everywhere.

It was only when John-Joe was saying goodbye to Crosby through the open window of the South-bound train that mention was made about the upcoming match.

"Uncle Joe, I'm playing in the match against The Rest of Ireland. It's the best way to understand what the new style game means to all of us."

There was no response.

"And," continued John-Joe, "you did ask me to find out all about it."

Crosby cleared his throat.

"You're right. Me and Quirk put you up to it. It's just that I don't want you to go over to Curran altogether."

"I'm not sure I will. But I have to try it."

"Be careful."

"Don't worry. I'll keep my elbows in."

Crosby shook his hands with unusual warmth as the train pulled out of the station.

12

"So it's no referees?" John-Joe was appalled.

"What's the matter Crosby?" Vinnie snarled at him. "Getting cold feet?"

Curran was presenting the final rules for the upcoming match. The players and support personnel were seated in the auditorium and the rules were projected on a screen behind Curran.

"We have dispensed with the referee," he said. "There will be a panel of adjudicators, to whom appeals will be made only in cases of serious injury. Besides, it will be too dangerous on the pitch for a referee."

The players cheered and slapped each other on the back. Only John-Joe seemed dismayed.

"Since serious injuries are… not unlikely," continued Curran "There is, as you can see, provision for ten substitutes. And here…" he cued another slide, "are your opponents."

The deep, disturbing soundtrack of male voices started and slowly increased in volume. Led by the Oriental men, the *Danann* began to growl and gesture at the photograph of The Rest of Ireland team. They all began to stamp their feet in a slow, inexorable rhythm. John-Joe took a look around. All their faces were contorted in hate. A group rage seemed to grip them, very like the group of drunks he had met last night. They were growling and gnashing their teeth. Foam and spittle began to flow from some of their mouths as they swayed and growled and hissed. It was horrible and John-Joe felt slightly sick. Curran let the emotion run for a while and then held up his hand. All was still again and the soundtrack was softer as he continued.

"There will be videos of each of those players shown later today. We have made an analysis of their strengths..." He paused for the scornful snorts.

"And their weaknesses."

The assembled men laughed and cheered.

"Study them well," shouted Curran. "This is the first game in Arena21 and the first hurling match of the modern era. I expect nothing less than total and absolute commitment. Those among you who do not give that commitment will be dropped from the team. Instantly and forever," he paused again, to let that sink in. Then he cued another slide and left the auditorium. It was a list of the chosen players for the match. John-Joe sought his name. It was as fourth substitute. Vinnie glanced across.

"It's all you're able for yet," he said.

John-Joe suspected he was right but he called back.

"Oh, I'll be in that match. Don't you worry."

That night Tim was among the millions watching the news on television. He hated the newsreader and hated even more the news that he was reading off his autocue.

"The long awaited hurling game between Jack Curran's Danann and The Rest of Ireland takes place on Saturday in Arena21. Bookmakers throughout the country are giving four to one in favour of the *Danann*. The on-line betting on the *Danann* website is reported to be heavy, with punters clicking on the site and betting at the rate of over a quarter of a million every day. We spoke to Mr Curran earlier today."

Curran appeared on screen.

"Our website can barely cope with the traffic," he said. "And an estimated twenty- million viewers will watch the *Danann* thrash the Rest of Ireland on the major TV channels in almost every country in the developed world. In the process they will make hurling a truly universal sport."

Tim switched channels. People were being interviewed on the streets.

"It'll kill the game," said one. "All that man cares about is the money."

"I'm looking forward to the new game," said another. "Remember when *Riverdance* happened? It changed Irish dancing forever. All the culchies were up in arms! Well (bleep) them! I'm all for something new."

"Our lovely game!" moaned a third. "Played by hooligans!"

A woman spoke next.

"It'll be great gas. Like the wrestling."

Tim switched channels again and the *Danann* TV commercial started to play. He turned off the TV in disgust. He felt bombarded. He thought that he had been singled out for news about the *Danann*. In fact he was a mere statistic, an anticipated recipient of one of the most-pervasive marketing and PR campaigns ever mounted. Curran had purchased McDonnells, the largest advertising agency in Ireland in anticipation of the campaign. He had replaced the entire creative staff with a team recruited from some of the world's most sophisticated mass-media and direct response companies and agencies. He had also head-hunted the marketing director of Microsoft, Harvey Switzer, the man responsible for the later world-wide launches of Windows in which the several updates of the software had been introduced to up to twenty countries on the same day.

Switzer was a brilliant, highly creative and ruthless little snot. His first action in taking over the agency was to fire all top management except financial. He then sought those men and women who believed, as he did, that, in marketing, absolutely nothing is left to chance. He was prepared to have the best creative brains spend as much time on the creation and production of a throwaway item as on a high-end television commercial. His demands for faultless excellence wreaked havoc with the egos, mental stability and ulcers of some of the highest-paid creatives in the business. He drove everybody to the extremes of their abilities, trampling on their self-esteem and professional pride with total disregard. That he wasn't physically assaulted daily was due to two factors; his PA without whom he never moved, was a six foot three black man with eyes as hard as the edges of his hands, and the salary and bonus cheques he handed out were legendary. Five seconds with his PA could be lethal and eighteen months of remuneration could literally set the recipient up for life.

Behind the scenes Switzer had been working on the *Danann* campaign for years. The media hype, which built to a crescendo generated two wide ranging and carefully orchestrated debates. On the global scale, the issue was the feasibility of hurling, an obscure sport, building an international following. As a catalyst, a series of slick promotional videos were screened on satellite channels worldwide. They equated hurling with the world's most favoured sports and drew complimentary parallels. It had the speed of tennis, as several tennis superstars proclaimed. It had the rough and tumble of rugby, according to many leading practitioners of that robust sport. Switzer was also party to Curran's secretive preparations for buying influence in any clubs which played Pelota, a Basque ball game played with futuristic hand-held curved baskets which propelled a small, extremely-hard ball at speeds in excess of 200 kph. A leading Chinese martial arts teacher had been recruited to extol the discipline required to play the new-style hurling on a series of TV shows and Curran was always on hand to throw in the ancient Celt aspect and to hark back to the glorious days of Ireland's supremacy. His interviews were invariably peppered with beautifully produced footage of the *Danann* at play. Rumour had it that Tommy Chin, Hollywood's hottest martial-arts director had been brought to Ireland incognito to shoot the commercials. Curran neither confirmed nor denied this.

The *Danann* website, with its swirling, mesmerising Celtic ornamentation and dramatic video clips of the members of the *Danann* team in action, attracted many millions of hits and persuaded punters from all over the world to bet on the outcome of the match. A streamed, interactive section of the site enabled the answering of FAQs and teams of facilitators engineered supposedly personal, and intensely interactive contact with the individual players. In an unprecedented and controversial deal, he had persuaded the Irish Post Office to issue a series of postage stamps in the more widely-used denominations featuring members of the *Danann* team. Orders for the first-day covers, to be released on the day of the match, poured in from all over the world.

There were many special offers in clothing and hurling equipment and a wide range of exciting giveaways for children and adults. Each article was designed to the Nth degree. Carefully thought out competitions were launched with valuable prizes to be won. Downloads were available of 'secret' manoeuvres by players and visitors to the site were invited to watch out for these in the first game and they could win prizes if they spotted and accurately timed the manoeuvres in the match. The *Danann* songs, recorded by the hottest Irish supergroup were available for downloading, as well as specially-composed music tracks.

In a brilliant marketing move, The *Danann* video game was released throughout key markets almost simultaneously and advertised heavily on television. North America, Western Europe, Australia and Mainland China saw the bulk of this campaign and sales soared in the weeks leading up to the game. In scope and scale, the multimedia campaign was as invasive and persuasive as anything Microsoft had ever devised and the world responded. Switzer held an auction of the broadcast rights via a global video conference and Sony paid the most to obtain the first game and they immediately sold it to broadcasters throughout the world. The fee paid for North American television rights was not disclosed and the successful network entered an agreement with a movie distributor to hold screenings on hi definition plasma screens in key theatres throughout the region. These screenings were to be the pivotal event in a day-long extravaganza which, thanks to the fact that the game was going to be played in the early hours of the morning in Dublin, made it a feasible broadcasting ploy across most of the United States, unfolding later and later on the day across the time zones. Curran was banking on the North American market not only for the audiences but as a catchment area for franchise hurling teams to participate in a planned international series throughout the year. His strong links with the large, influential Irish-American societies lay good groundwork for that project.

There was more money generated in the pre-match period than the Olympics had ever engendered and sports administrators and broadcasters everywhere went green with envy and frantically looked around for an indigenous sport of their own to promote. Sony had exclusive ownership of the branding of the event and their logo appeared on anything even remotely connected with the match but, to their chagrin, advertising airtime during the game, restricted to one single sixty-second commercial, to be screened immediately prior to the play off, was put out to open tender. Every major advertising agency in the world bid for that spot on behalf of their major clients. Switzer declared himself the sole judge of the most suitable script and storyboard and the competition was frenetic. The world's agencies and production companies and commercial directors and producers and cinematographers clamoured to work on the production, for nothing if necessary. They needn't have bothered. The production budget allocated to the winning commercial was greater than the GDP of several respectable countries and there was money enough for every commercial effort and CGI effect known to the industry. The winner of the bid was a sporting footwear company working out of Wisconsin called "The Great American Shoe Company". The script and storyboard had been submitted on their behalf by an ex-South African commercials director who had come up with a beautiful concept and had persuaded the shoe manufacturer to use the opportunity – and the advert – to achieve immediate No.2 slot in that lucrative but highly competitive market. Switzer was enthusiastic about the concept when he informed Curran of his decision in the plush Fitzwilliam Square premises of McDonnells. His office was dominated by an enormous rosewood table bearing a laptop, three framed photographs of him with three consecutive American presidents, an intercom connected to every room in the building (every room – "Don't think a crap on *my* time is a moment of private communion between you and your asshole!") and a crumpled bullet in a cube of acrylic glass.

"It's a great TV concept," he told Curran. "Not only is it hideously expensive, a necessary prerequisite, but it involves smartass endorsements from the top, I mean *top* players in almost every goddam sport under the sun."

"It *will* help our positioning," Curran ventured.

"Goddam right. And position, as the Anglican assbandit said, *apropos* of the rubberassed choir boy, is everything," Switzer gestured at the storyboard which was pinned on the wall. "He has the players in hell, for fuck sake! Interviewed by the devil! The man's mad, but a genius. He'll offend every religious jerk on the planet and *they'll* make sure that every jerk-off artist in this vale of fucking tears gets to hear about and seek out and react to the commercial. We'll have this ad quoted, chapter and verse, from every fucking pulpit on this mortal coil. Shit! I'll hire the bastard when the match is over."

Curran respected dedication and Switzer's dedication was overwhelming. His meetings with his communications expert left him dazed. He, who dealt in concrete things and the comforting miasma of balance sheets, was somewhat daunted by the perpetual cliff-hanging of this ferocious person who rode his emotions and impressions like a rodeo champion. When told by Switzer how much the Great American Shoe Company was paying for the production and screening of the commercial, he had blanched slightly.

"What if it doesn't work?"

"Not my problem. Not your problem. Not the *Danann's* problem. Funny things, ads. They can catch the imagination and fucking *force* people out to buy. Or they can whistle by unnoticed. Doesn't matter how good they are, how expensive they are or how well researched they are. This is a good one, though and I guess it'll shift a shitload of shoes. Dig the slogan," he indicated the storyboard "'the killer sport shoe from the great American Shoe Company'. That'll work, especially given the... attrition... of the game, hey?"

So Curran had left Switzer to his devices and relied on weekly planning meetings to co-ordinate the marketing with the training and stadium building.

13

With Sony's funding, Curran and his technical team threw everything at the match. Fifty state-of-the-art hi-definition cameras covered the field itself and another 150 covered the dressing room, the corridors and the immediate environs. Three drones carried cameras and six more were strung across and along the pitch. A feed from every camera went not only for satellite and selected terrestrial transmission but to the security complex on top of the stands. An enormous media control room had been incorporated into the design of the stadium overlooking the pitch and a week before the match, it was fully connected and crammed with equipment, technicians and commentators.

The gates opened in the early evening with entertainment by a galaxy of celebrities and three musical groups, starting with a big swing band, moving through orchestral lollipops played by the National Symphony Orchestra and ending with a rock super-group. The next slot was an Irish dancing, multimedia experience, complete with three-dimensional holographic dancers who hovered, larger than life, above the ground at midfield. The stadium was filled to capacity by midnight and an hour later, the lights suddenly went out. In the darkness, the first powerful beats of the *Danann* hymn started. Curran had commissioned the music according to the most up-to-date psychological data on motivational music and the opus by a leading Hollywood composer owed much to Vangelis who has been responsible for many twentieth-century movie themes. It was an intoxicating blend of deep male voices, a throbbing bass beat and a sparkling string and brass theme floating over all. A curtain of water, created by thousands of jets along the sideline, shot in bursts fifteen metres into the air and in time to the music. Over a hundred powerful video projectors on the roofs of the stands, cast images of swirling Celtic patterns onto the water curtain. The crowd gasped and cheered as the patterns shifted and shimmered all around the pitch. At a choral passage in the music, two enormous plasma screens, one at each end of the stadium, filled with *Danann* imagery and action. As the stirring tune increased in intensity, six enormous helicopters descended on the field and hovered twenty metres above the pitch.

The water curtain diminished as coloured straps fell from each helicopter. Sliding down the straps came the *Danann* team one by one. As each landed, his picture appeared on the screens and his real name and carefully chosen nickname was announced. A bevy of lovely young women, dressed in *Danann* colours ran onto the pitch, each carrying a hurley. They ran across to the players and handed each his stick before running off again. There was a pause as the crowd waited to see how the Rest of Ireland team would enter. It was not disappointed. Slowly one end of the pitch opened upwards. Beams of laser and other light stabbed the sky and swirling dry ice flowed onto the grass as the opening grew deeper. To the strains of a mediocre, brass band hymn, out of the gap came a succession of chariots, each drawn by a cloaked figure on a three-wheeled motorbike with wide, pneumatic wheels to protect the turf. They were as gladiatorial as you could ask for. A blonde woman in a white toga held the reins of each chariot and standing behind each one was a player in a bright green outfit and an orange cloak. Each held a hurley stretched forward above the driver's head. The chariots drew to a stop before the line of *Danann* and each player dismounted and took up his position in a similar line-up facing them. The chariots wheeled away and disappeared down the opening which slowly closed.

Silence fell. A countdown clock appeared on each screen. The players ran to take up their positions. A klaxon blared as zero was reached and a glowing hurling ball was shot from a hidden catapult and landed in the exact centre of the pitch.

The game was on and the crowd went wild.

The *Danann* were silent, incredibly precise and ruthless. Immediately their carefully-devised movements allowed them to reach the other goal as if the rest of Ireland team wasn't there. The first goal was scored with almost contemptuous ease and the Rest of Ireland team and the crowd was stunned into silence.

Vinnie had scored the goal. He threw his hurley into the air in triumph and it turned, glistening in the floodlights. The crowd took its cue from him and roared its approval. The Rest of Ireland took the sixty-second break allowed for in the new rules and key players huddled together and consulted while a holograph of the score hovered in mid-air above the field. Both teams took up position and the ball was pucked in by the rest of Ireland's goalie. This time they were readier for the swift *Danann* attack. Vinnie, in centre field caught the ball on his stick and passed it to an already sprinting player on the wing. Two Rest of Ireland players tackled him, slammed him over the sideline and took the ball from him. One of them moved toward the *Danann* goal but three *Danann* players were onto him like tigers. The slam of four bodies colliding was audible all over the field and the *Danann,* firmly in possession, moved towards their opponents' goal. The Rest of Ireland player they had tackled was left upright and remarkably still for several seconds. Then he crumpled senseless to the ground but very few eyes were on him. A rash Rest of Ireland player moved to meet the *Danann* and took the full brunt of two of them as they hurled themselves at him at full speed. He was slammed to the ground and one *Danann* landed on his chest while the other landed across his thighs. The crack of breaking bones was audible as the third leaped over their heads and ran towards goal, with other *Dananns* moving up on either side of him. He scored with ease as the crowd murmured uneasily.

Several medics rushed onto the field and carted off the two Rest of Ireland players as the *Danann* took up their places silently. The Rest of Ireland, supplemented by two substitutes, took full advantage of the full sixty seconds and, as the klaxon signalled the break end, they moved into their places with a grim determination.

This time it was more even. The Rest of Ireland players seemed more focussed on hurting the *Danann* than gaining possession of the ball. However, in spite of their increased efforts, the next score was by a *Danann* and a fervour seemed to grip every Rest of Ireland player on the field. They played like men demented and, such was the mood swing of the crowd, that it roared its approval of every successful Rest of Ireland move and booed and screamed at the *Danann*. When the Rest of Ireland scored the next goal, the crowd was on its feet. As the scorer ran to the sideline to acknowledge the approval, he passed close to a *Danann* who almost casually chopped his kneecap with his hurley and loped back to centre field as the stricken player dropped to the ground, his kneecap obviously smashed.

The mood of the crowd changed again. A howl of outrage rose from the stands and a spectator leaped to his feet and ran to the barrier around the stand. He snatched a drinks can from his pocket and threw it at the guilty *Danann* who was standing facing the crowd, eyeing it impassively. The can, obviously full, approached his head. He caught it, opened the tab and threw it straight back at the crowd. There was some uneasy laughter, some groans and some howls of anger as the can, spewing its contents, descended on the stands. All this was hushed as several black uniformed security guards moved in on the man who had first thrown the can. He was yelling abuse at the *Danann* and didn't see them coming. An electric prod was jammed under his arm. He convulsed and collapsed into the grip of the guards. Silently they carried him away, his head lolling at an angle, his limbs flopping. Within seconds, the guards had disappeared into an opening among the seats, leaving an angry and dismayed crowd. The next goal was scored by Vinnie who began to dominate the match from his centre forward position. He loped through it all like a lone wolf, springing into action every time the ball came near, tackling with ferocity any opponent who invaded his space.

When the half-time klaxon blared, the Rest of Ireland team had called eight substitutes onto the field and the *Danann* three. Confused noises rose from the crowd as the players, many of them limping, left the pitch. Several fights broke out in the stands but these were quickly and brutally quelled by the security guards who belaboured all the fighters with equal impartiality and a great deal of relish. Mostly, however, the crowd had been swept along by the undoubtedly exciting mayhem on the pitch and, if they were subdued during half-time they, nevertheless, were eager to see the game recommence. The security guards had become increasingly in evidence now as they patrolled up and down the wide paths between the blocks of seats eyeing the crowd closely. Some of the crowd left their seats and headed towards the refreshment stands which had been stocked only with soft drinks.

The *Dananns* were leading by three goals to two at the break and many of the commentators in the media room were hoarsely reviewing the first part of the game to listeners and viewers all over the world. Curran had been pacing the room, watching the match and the viewership figures with equal interest and increasing satisfaction. Feedback from the various channels indicated that the ratings were growing as the game went on. It was clear that even the mighty audience ratings for the Olympic Games were being surpassed. On the website, comments were pouring in as visitors expressed both fascination and disgust in equal proportions. Curran was unperturbed, knowing that the real fans, engrossed in the game, would not tear themselves away from their sets while the match was in progress. Most of the adverse comments, he surmised, were from people who had stopped watching and subsequent events proved him right. Analysis of the traffic to the website indicated that the vast majority of the negative comments were from people who had switched off in horror. The visitors to the site who identified the 'secret' manoeuvres of the *Danann* were legion and their names were captured for the prize-giving session which would be held after the final klaxon.

The mood in both dressing rooms was sombre. Most of the *Dananns* were subdued by the level of violence which had exceeded their expectations. Vinnie alone seemed in his element. He moved around the dressing room, congratulating the more ferocious of his teammates and encouraging the waverers. He had done much to restore morale when Curran came in and got down to business without any preamble.

"You are not playing hard enough," he said when he had got their attention. "It is essential that you strike total fear into their hearts. When you go back onto the field, the klaxon will sound immediately, before they are ready. Each of you will, without a moment's delay, tackle the man next to him. Terror shall rule this half. They will be so afraid of each of you that they will not be able to concentrate on tactics or scoring. I want their last two substitutes used up and I want to see their numbers reduced, to the last man if possible and then I want to see him fall with a broken head. Do I make myself clear?"

Even Vinnie was momentarily taken aback by his venom but he recovered quickly.

"Don't worry, Mr Curran," he said. "That first half was just practice. We were saving it up for the second half. We'll do for them. Won't we, lads?"

He and Curran looked around. Most of them, white faced nodded. John-Joe felt trapped. There was no way he wanted to play at this level of vehemence but nor was there any way he could get out of it. Deep, deep down, he wanted to find out if he could be as ruthless as this game required. He looked at the stiffening resolve of his teammates and decided he had to play and he knew that the two subs who stood between him and playing would soon be carried off.

The Rest of Ireland team was perturbed by the injuries inflicted on the players who had been carried off and the two remaining two substitutes were exceedingly nervous, having seen the injured players close up. Their coach tried, half-heartedly to give them a pep talk but the words died on his lips. They all sat slumped in a state bordering on shock, waiting for the second half with the resignation of men going to their deaths. The coach looked around at them and realised that nothing he said would have any effect on their resolve – or lack of it.

Curran had been correct. The two teams came back onto the pitch and took up their positions. At the first sound of the klaxon, before the propelled ball had landed, each *Danann* moved in on his mark facing him and tried to fell him with either a blow from a hurley or a vicious body blow. The crowd howled at the shamelessness of it but when Vinnie scooped up the ball and ran unimpeded towards goal, the animal instinct took over and they greeted his score with a raucous acclaim. The klaxon signalled a break and the medics ran on with their stretchers. Most of the Rest of Ireland players had been caught totally off guard and were stretched on the turf. Some however, had returned the assault with deadly effect and two *Dananns* were also down. John-Joe was on.

He ran onto the field with mixed emotions. Gratuitous violence was against everything he stood for. Playing hurling hard but fair was the major lesson of his life, instilled at childhood and nurtured throughout his young life. He had never tried to deliberately hurt anyone, not even in his unthinking childhood years when his natural exuberance and sense of mischief had brought him up against other children in schoolyard and back street scraps. Now here he was going amongst nearly thirty men inflamed by anger and hate, with very little evidence of fair play and no chance of intervention in the case of extreme violence. If he thought passions were high as he viewed the field from the sidelines, it was nothing to the umbra of danger and rage through which he ran to his position. Every face was twisted in anger. Every eye glared at him as he passed. Every player – on both teams – seethed almost at boiling point, as if one move from him would send them over the edge into murderous behaviour, with him as the victim. The sense of evil was palpable and his heart shrank as he reached the forward line and waited for the ball to be lobbed in. He was on Vinnie's left and he caught his eye as he crouched forward, ready for action. Vinnie's look was sardonic.

"OK Kerryboy. Show us what you're made of."

The klaxon sounded and the ball dropped to the ground. Sensing Vinnie's surge forward, John-Joe ran automatically down the wing, feeling confident that the ball would come his way. It was a long, beautiful pass from Vinnie, coming to earth at precisely the right distance. Lengthening his stride, he scooped it easily onto his stick and all his instincts came automatically into play. He swerved away from the body which he sensed was coming at him from infield and tumbled head over heels as a hurley caught his ankle, fortunately on the edge of his shin guard. As he rolled forwards to displace the energy of the fall, he saw a boot coming straight at his face. He willed an increase in his momentum and managed to roll way from the trajectory of the boot. It was barely enough. The boot missed his eye and landed on his helmet with a force that almost snapped his neck. A dark shape flew over his body and connected with the player who had kicked him. There was a whoosh of air as a pair of lungs collapsed and the dark shape rolled over the fallen body and rolled towards the goal, rising upright with impressive grace. It was Vinnie, heading for his third goal. He scored it and ran back towards his place, passing John-Joe on the way. John-Joe caught his eye, ready to nod his thanks but changed his mind when Vinnie hissed.

"Wake up for fuck's sake."

He ran past and John-Joe followed to the centre of the pitch. So this was how it was going to be? Right, he'd give as good as he got. He crouched in position, pushing from his mind the image of that nearly lethal boot.

Only one moment remained clear in his mind in the midst of that awful second half, in the midst of men almost driven mad by violence and counter-violence, by slashes given and thuds taken, by the crash of bodies and the clawing of hands, arms and hurleys. By the screams of rage and the moans of injury. He had received the ball on the left wing and balancing it on his hurley, he ran for the goal. Four Rest of Ireland men were in a loose line in front of him. He swerved as if to pass them on the inside but, turning on his heel, he slammed the ball at the head of the man on the right who stopped and leaned back to catch the ball on his stick. Tucking his elbows well into his sides, John-Joe glided through the men and, reaching back, he scooped the ball off the man's stick. There was an open goal before him and pivoting to his right he flipped the ball into the air and as it descended, caught it on the sweetest spot of the hurley boss. The ball soared through the goal mouth, a split second before the final klaxon sounded, with the *Danann* three goals in the lead.

Instead of the jubilation which usually followed a hard-fought match, an overwhelming sense of unease imbued every man on the pitch. Oblivious of the crowd's roaring, the men of both teams filed off the pitch in silence. As for the crowd, it was delirious. Those sickened by the brutality had left long ago and there had been few enough of them anyway. The remainder was excited beyond the experience of any sports official at the game. Bloodlust was not too strong a name for the emotion that had taken over during the second half. There was none of the partisanship which might have been expected from so strongly a promoted match. The crowd had called for blood and both teams had delivered. At the end of the game, all substitutes had been called on field and subsequent to that eight men had been carried off. The crowd lauded the remainder much as the surviving gladiators had been lauded by the Romans so many centuries ago.

Curran, from his vantage point above the field, knew he had tapped into the darker recesses of the human mind and had struck a chord of animal satisfaction at the witnessing of both deep suffering and heroic endeavour. Around him, the commentators from all over the world were summing up the match to their audiences in a fever of excitement. He moved over to the computer console and scanned the pages of the website that were displayed. They were rapidly scrolling as inputs came in about the game. Winning bets were being paid out, correctly identified manoeuvres were being examined and fervently-favourable comments were being posted from almost every country in the world. Reflecting on the remarkable vindication of his notions of the universal attraction of unbridled mayhem, Curran made his way towards the dressing rooms.

14

The sound was turned down on Mrs Ring's television but the pictures were self explanatory; selected scenes from the match, the scoreboard, the crowd, and, most of all, Curran's gloating face, flushed with satisfaction as he was interviewed. Kitty and Mrs Ring were sitting silently, watching the set, wrapped in their own thoughts when the front door opened and footsteps approached the kitchen.

A moment later, John-Joe was in the room, a plaster on his forehead, a bunch of roses and a bottle of whiskey in his grasp and an expectant look on his face. The last faded at the sight of Kitty's stony face.

"I think," she said slowly. "You'd better look for somewhere else to stay."

She stood up and moved towards the door. John-Joe offered the flowers. She looked at them expressionlessly and walked past him. John-Joe looked at Mrs Ring who sighed and turned up the volume on the TV. John-Joe placed the flowers and whiskey on the table.

"Well," he said. "I'll start looking tomorrow."

He left and Mrs Ring sighed again.

Larry King was interviewing Curran on the TV.

"Rumour has it," intoned King, "that you're about to start a hurling team in Dallas, with one of the producers of the TV series, *Dallas* as the main backer."

"I can't confirm or deny that," replied Curran. "But I intend to establish hurling teams throughout North America. In fact, recruiting has already started. This is the sport of the future."

"Some would say that play such as this should not be allowed in sport of any kind."

On the screen came a scene from the match. In slow motion, A *Danann* player flew through the air and crashed his shoulder into the face of a player from the rest of Ireland team. The latter's head snapped back and he crumpled to the ground, the hurley falling from his suddenly limp hand. The *Danann* landed on top of him and, as he rolled off, he dug his hurley into the man's groin and used it as a lever to get to his feet. The look of agony of the downed man's face showed that the usual box protection was ineffective. Larry King was at his most sincere.

"Now that is not sport."

"I agree and, if the Rest of Ireland team representative had protested, the panel of adjudicators would have penalised that player."

"Mr Curran, the rules and the training for this form of hurling encourage that sort of dangerous tackling and—"

"Of course they do. I'm the first to admit that this is a dangerous sport. I was referring to the hurley in the groin of a downed man. That is forbidden under the new rules and that *Danann* player, would have been penalised, if an objection had been lodged."

"But with the general level of mayhem on the field would make this sort of play the rule rather than the exception."

"I disagree. My players are very disciplined. They are trained to remain emotionally disengaged while on the field. They know how to keep their cool."

“Well,” said King. “That player certainly kept what you refer to as ‘his cool’. Moments later, this is what he did to another opponent.”

A second clip showed the same player jumping for the ball. He turned in mid- air as his hurley connected with the ball and snap-kicked the other player high in the chest. This player too slumped to the ground.

“Now that’s hardly sportsmanlike behaviour. Its mayhem made respectable,” said King.

“So is professional boxing and most forms of wrestling,” Curren countered. “Look at Rugby League as played in the North of England. That’s as brutal as you can get off a battlefield. I’m sorry. My style of hurling is violent, sure. And that’s its major attraction.”

Mrs Ring switched channels in disgust. She tuned into a business report to see a German being interviewed. On the screen behind him was a *Danann* image. The businessman was responding to a question put to him in the studio.

“We have founded a hurling school in Mannheim so there will be a strong hurling capability in Germany before the year is finished.”

She switched channels back to an Irish station and saw a worried priest addressing an interviewer.

“I think,” he said, “that this game has tapped into the darkest recesses of the human psyche. I would advocate excommunication but…” he sighed. “I’m afraid those days are over.”

She switched again and caught another interview, this time with an American.

“I intend to establish hurling teams in every major city. I own the franchise throughout North America and I’m recruiting right now. This is the sport of the future.”

“Merciful heavens,” said Mrs Ring, “where’s it all going to end?”

The next morning Kitty accessed the web on her computer at work and visited the *Danann* website. On the spectacular home page, she clicked on a picture of Curran. He immediately spoke.

"I own the broadcasting rights to this game in all media in seventeen regions around the world," the tinny voice said. "I provide fast-track training for all nations at the *Danann* headquarters here in Dublin."

She clicked on the button marked 'Players' and scrolled through the photographs until she came to one of John-Joe. She clicked on the name 'JJ Crosby' with a heavy heart. The photograph animated and John-Joe's voice issued from the speakers.

"It was luck really. The ball found me in the right place. Anyway, we didn't really need that goal. It was a great game, though."

"Oh, JJ," said Kitty aloud.

"That's me."

She turned to see John-Joe standing at the doorway.

"Great game," she said sarcastically.

"Yes. Great game."

"Seven men in hospital! Two of them will never play again!"

"Yes. Well. It's a pity about them."

"The whole game was pitiless. It was like… like a Roman circus with gladiators. The crowd wanted someone dead and they very nearly got its wish."

"Ah, come on. Nobody died."

"That wasn't Curran's fault. He's created a… a pack of wild animals. It was horrible. It's not a sport."

"It's no worse than ice hockey or boxing, or fight clubs, or any of the extreme sports," said John-Joe, beginning to get angry. "Those men, the other team, they weren't trained properly, that's why they got hurt."

Kitty closed down the computer and took up her bag, heading for the door.

"You mean they weren't trained to play dirty."

"There's a difference between dirty play and hard play," said John-Joe following her through the door. She ignored him and crossed the reception and into the street.

"I've seen enough dirty play on the GAA circuit. And men hurt too. Badly," he said to her back. "At least in this game you expect the worst and prepare for it."

"I don't want to hear any more about your bloody game."

"But you might want to know more about Tomas."

That stopped her. She turned and looked earnestly at him without speaking.

"Remember I joined the *Danann* because Uncle Joe asked me to. To find out if it will kill the old game or not."

"And will it?" she asked, in spite of herself.

"I don't know. It's too early. Maybe it's just a nine-day wonder, like reality TV. Maybe there's room for both different styles, like rugby league, rugby union and American football."

She shook her head impatiently.

"What about Tomas?"

"I told you I'd try to find out if there's any connection. But to do that I have to earn Curran's trust."

"Why should he trust you?"

"I'm one of his bright hopes right now and he loves to have strong men around him. When he's not blathering on about samurai and Celtic warriors, he's very open about his plans for the game and the stadium."

"Open? Him?"

"Well it's more like boasting. But he does speak about the politicians he has in his pocket. He doesn't care who knows it."

She stood there undecided for a while.

"I hate the game," she finally said. "But if you can find anything about Tomas, I… I'd be grateful."

15

John-Joe had always enjoyed circuses and fairs, like most children in his area. Unlike most children, however, he had separated in his mind those acts, displays and exhibitions that had some genuine skill attached to them from those that were slick and superficial and required only a modicum of ability to perform. The bareback horse riders, for example, didn't impress him. He thought the wide rump of an easily cantering horse a very secure platform on which to stand or jump or gyrate. He himself could stand upright on the saddle of his bike and steer it in figures of eight and ever-decreasing circles with the weight of his body, so he understood the relative ease of such capers. The trapeze artists were another thing altogether. Not the swinging. That looked simple and easy enough to master with practice but the triple swing into the hands of the catcher – that looked decidedly difficult and genuinely dangerous.

Most of the slot machines he found boring but the older machines, which had levers with genuine traction and resistance, he became skilled at. There was one machine which, for a penny, allowed you to flick a steel ball up onto a series of pins. Underneath the pins was a little carriage which could

LEABHARLANN CO. CILL DARA

be moved back and forth, to catch the ball as it fell through, glancing off the pins. If caught in the carriage, the ball went on to release a packet of five cigarettes. John-Joe understood the mechanism and became so adept that he supplied most of his peers and several older boys with a packet of fags for a penny. Until, that is, the attendant caught onto him and refused him access to the machine.

The clowns were beneath contempt but really strong men he admired. He despised punch-drunk professional boxers who, by their resistance to pain and their well-practised, automatic technique, could demolish the fresh-faced young locals who dared to climbed into the ring to face them. Supposedly grotesque or deformed humans or animals, he had no time for nor for the inept magicians who performed tawdry tricks in the dim light of tents and read the minds of their planted accomplices, to the gasps of the equally-dim audiences. One attraction which had always excited him was the globe of death. It involved two motorcyclists roaring around the inside of a mesh globe which was barely big enough to contain them. The big bikes thundered around at right angles to each other, the riders' heads inches apart in the centre of the globe. Faster and faster they went until the tent, reeking with exhaust fumes, shook and strained against its guy ropes. He always came out of the tent with his ears ringing and his heart pounding. The precision of the rotating bikes and the thought of what would happen if they did collide left him breathless. So when he saw the mesh globe in the *Danann* gym, the same sizes as the globe of death but with finer mesh, it evoked the smell and the noise and the excitement instantly.

This time, he was to enter the globe with Vinnie. The enmity between the two of them had become palpable, raising the stakes of any activity when they were opposed to each other. This time, they each wore crash helmets and carried hurleys as they clambered up into the globe and stood to one side as the gate was closed securely beneath them. They both took up positions facing each other and as far up the curve of the globe as they could go and still stand easily on their feet. The other team members gathered around the globe in silent anticipation. A bell sounded and a metal ball clunked in through a hole at the top. The bell was a micro second before the dropping ball but it was enough for Vinnie. He flicked it around the cage with a powerful swing of both arms. With the same momentum, he launched himself at John-Joe, slamming him onto the mesh in the path of the whizzing ball. John-Joe rolled with the fall and shifted onto his feet, just as the metal ball passed through the space where his head had been.

This time he got to the ball first and snapped it through the air at Vinnie. Vinnie ducked and twirled to get his stick to the ball. Again the flick around the cage, again the body-slam and this time the ball connected with John-Joe's shoulder. His arm went immediately numb and he almost dropped the stick. Vinnie grinned wolfishly and dived on the ball again sent it on an orbit towards John-Joe's feet. It caught him on the heel as he was bracing himself on the slope of the cage and his balance was just off centre. Down he went onto the bottom of the cage but the pain in his shoulder had metamorphosed into rage. He kept on rolling and used the momentum generated by the roll to clamber up towards the top of the cage. He hooked the handle of his hurley into the mesh and hung there for only a split second but it was enough to confuse Vinnie who turned towards where John-Jo would have been had he continued. John-Joe released himself and fell onto Vinnie, slamming him the bottom with stunning force. This gave him time to reach the ball which was still moving around the mesh but dropping as it slowed down. He hooked his hurley behind the ball, speeding it on its way towards the bottom and Vinnie, grunting with satisfaction as it connected with Vinnie's hip.

They both paused, panting as the ball settled on the bottom. Then Vinnie tore off his helmet and spurted up the slope of the globe. He thrust the helmet through the hole at the top and then fell to the bottom, landing lightly on both feet and glaring at John-Joe. John-Joe paused for the slightest time before he also divested himself of his helmet and sent it out through the hole, dropping down to land crouching on the lower slope.

Vinnie was closer to the ball this time and got to it first but John-Joe was now playing for keeps. He launched himself at Vinnie, sending him crashing into the mesh, just as he flicked the ball around the globe. This time, John-Joe's roll happened directly in the path of the speeding ball, and at precisely the same time. The ball connected with the back of his head and his world went dark. Grinning in triumph, Vinnie scooped the ball onto his stick and was about to flick it straight at John-Joe's head when an icy voice cut through the apprehensive buzz of the watching players.

"That's enough." It was an angry Curran.

The bottom of the globe dropped open and John-Joe fell through onto the ground where he sat groggily for a few seconds and Vinnie leapt out over him, stepping on his thigh as he did so.

"Anything broken?" asked Curran.

"No," muttered John-Joe as he got to his feet.

"Now listen to me. You are my property and I'm willing to risk your well-being in a match but not in the gym."

They both stood silent in front of him. Curran suddenly grinned and punched both of them of the shoulder.

"You tigers," he said. "Save that lovely aggression for the matches. OK?"

As Curran walked off, Vinnie and John-Joe glared at each other. Vinnie stepped close to John-Joe and angled his head as he thrust it to within an inch of John-Joe's.

"Soon, Culchie, it'll be just you and me on a pitch, then we'll see who's a tiger and who's a pussycat," he hissed.

"I can't wait," said John-Joe.

Switzer had excelled himself for the press conference. It was held in a marquee in the stadium and packaged in a slick, exciting and entertaining way. Two giant balloons were tethered above each of the goal posts and onto them was projected images of the inaugural match, with music and sound effects played in total surround sound from speakers above all the stands. A dancing sequence was performed on a raised stage at the centre field and a jazz band played alternately on a stage on the main stand. The performances were also projected onto the balloons. The food, the drinks, the service was superb and all the *Dananns* were there, in specially designed leisure suits in the corporate colours. When the audio-visuals and the dancing were completed, the guests were invited to take their seats inside the marquee in front of an enormous screen.

Curran stared the proceedings by introducing the video link-ups to North Dublin, where several GAA office bearers were gathered and to an hotel in Kerry, where the managers of the Kerry team were assembled. Curran welcomed the participants, acknowledging most of them by name and then proceeded;

"Hurling is no longer an obscure, parochial pastime for a few-thousand people. It is poised to become, indeed, has already become, after only one match, a vibrant, exciting, world-class sport. It will generate passion, partisanship and loyalty among millions of people at live venues around the world and amongst billions of viewers on TV and on the internet. Our inaugural game demonstrated some of the potential and now it is time for the first true test of the game. I challenge Kerry, the current All-Ireland hurling champions to a game under the new hurling rules at Arena21. This will determine, once and for all, supremacy in Ireland's age-old and the world's newest super sport."

A buzz ran around the audience and the panels on both screens exchanged looks and murmurs. Curran waited for a moment before addressing the screens.

"Gentlemen of the Gaelic Athletic Association, are you prepared to sanction this match and to acknowledge the winner as the new All-Ireland champions?"

A tall, gangly man on one of the screens leaned forward.

"*Is mise Tomas Mac Mathuna, Uachtaran an Cumann Luathcleas Gael.* I'm Tom MacMahon, president of the Gaelic Athletic Association. *Is sinne a thugann ceadunas don cluiche idit DeDannan agus Countai Ciarrai, curaidh na hEireann.* We sanction this match between the *Danann* and the Kerry champions. However, the GAA reserves the right to the All-Ireland title for the more traditional style of playing. *Iomanaiocht clasaiceach a tabharfar ar seo.* Which we will call Classic Hurling. *Ta an sochru seo do-aistrithe.* That is non-negotiable."

Curran bit his lip and conferred briefly with two men who stood close to him. An excited murmur ran through the crowd of journalists and dignitaries. Curran again faced the screen.

"Mr MacMahon, surely the winner of this match will have proved that they are indeed, the champions?"

"The winners of this match will be entitled to call themselves Irish Champions, New Style Hurling. The All-Ireland title will be reserved exclusively for those teams which play in the traditional, classic style. That is our final decision."

On one of the screens, Joe Crosby coughed nervously and tapped the microphone in front of him.

"Em. Can you hear me? Can you—"

"We hear you loud and clear, Mr Crosby," said Curran. "You have been the custodian of Kerry's reputation and honour for many years. Do you have a mandate to accept this challenge?"

"I do. Subject to the terms my GAA President has explained," said Joe then, with another cough, he continued. "We have been aware of your intention to challenge Kerry and it has caused much debate and soul-searching down here in Kerry and indeed, all over Ireland."

"And the result of that debate?" asked Curran.

“The result is that the current all-Ireland champions of Classic Hurling accept the challenge.” said Joe. He coughed once more and sat down.

Gritting his teeth, Curran acknowledged the decision and went on to specify the time and date of the match, before facing the questions from the journalists. As John-Joe left the marquee, he passed Vinnie talking to some players. Vinnie caught his eye.

“We’ll teach those fucking culchies, once and for all,” he said loudly.

John-Joe waked on without comment. He had to find Tim and do some bridge building.

16

"And you're going to be captain!" Tim was furious and incredulous and the mélange of emotions had him confused. But mostly he was hurt. He strode away and headed in among the chestnut trees that spread their mighty canopies up into the pellucid air. John-Joe let him go and followed at a more leisurely pace. He had walked silently listening as Tim poured invective on him; for joining Curran, for playing in the terrible match, for deserting Tim and the classic sport which they both loved so much. He had known that Tim would be upset and torn in his loyalties and had chosen the Phoenix Park for the confrontation, knowing that the broad, beautiful environs would sooth Tim's troubled breast. He caught up with him knowing that he was on a trigger edge and would explode again if John-Joe wasn't careful.

"Tim. Tim. Listen to me carefully. Understand what I'm telling you. I didn't undertake this lightly and I have spoken at length to Uncle Joe and MacMahon. We worked this out together."

"MacMahon?"

"Yes. The president. He's a very shrewd man and he saw this

coming. Inevitable he said it was. What we're doing is for the good of the game."

"The good of the game!"

"Yes. MacMahon has had this plan up his sleeve for years. Ever since he first heard of Curran and his intentions. He's been travelling the world, meeting top people in soccer, tennis and particularly rugby. All those sports have been through some sort of revolution and – this is important – they all survived. Even thrived."

"Yeah, well..." Tim was reluctant to give him any argument space.

"Take rugby. There was a big split, two in fact, in the space of a hundred years. The first was when Rugby League and Rugby Union parted company and the rules and the status of player changed. The second was when the Americans took over football and rugby and devised their own versions, some tougher than others. All three are thriving and all three are professional. And see how cricket has evolved to suit the broadcasters' demands with One Day Innings. Don't tell me they ruined the game by being more popular than the five day – five day! – test matches."

"I know all that."

"Well, then see the similarities between those sports and hurling. They evolved and so will hurling. Tennis too. Look how that has grown in popularity – without affecting club tennis, except for increasing *its* popularity. But – and this is the important thing – behind the up-front, gung-ho, spectacular showing off, with power drives and hairy-chested tackles by men mountains, the real, refined versions of the sports have survived and built up a solid base of players who might admire the spectacular TV capers but would never aspire to them. They look for finesse, delicacy, subtlety and skill. The things that make sport so attractive."

"What does Curran have to say about you playing for Kerry?" Tim asked.

"He doesn't know it. Yet. But I don't think he'll mind so much."

"But you know too much about their methods."

"That won't bother him. The more evenly the two teams are matched, the happier he'll be. Providing, of course, the *Danann* win."

"And if they do, you'll have wasted your time."

"Tim," sighed John-Joe. "Don't you see, it's not as cut and dried as winning or losing. It's more about skill against brutality. About the finer points of hurling, not the crude mayhem the *Danann* are good at. That mayhem is their main selling point and if I have my way, it'll be their downfall."

"Does Curran know anything about this? About the way you feel?"

"I don't know. I suppose he does. It all adds to the drama of the match and that's all he cares about. Tim, I'm going to save the game."

"You? How?"

"By showing that the classic game is ultimately more satisfying to watch and more rewarding to play. But I'll need all the skill I can recruit. I'll need a team of dedicated players who can face the *Danann* and through sheer skill and fine hurling, give them a good run for their money."

"They can't be beaten."

"Maybe. I've been there, inside their dark hearts. I know their skills and their weaknesses. With players like you I can and will create space and opportunities in the coming game for fine play to happen and to be seen by the watchers, in the stadium and on the broadcasts. I'll give them more classy moves to admire and more complex manoeuvres to demonstrate that there is more to this fucking game than bone crunching and bloody limbs. Hey. Look what I've found."

It was a length of rusty iron, lying in the long grass. John-Joe picked it up and weighed it in his hand.

"Nothing's changed. I used to have a bar just like this."

He leaned backwards and hurled the iron bar at a particularly attractive cluster of chestnuts in the mighty tree. The bar connected with the slender twig from which the chestnuts dangled seductively. It was a well thrown bar and the cluster dropped to the ground. Both men pounced on them and split the vivid green capsules open to expose the shiny brown conkers which lay glistening and pristine in their palms.

"So clean," Tim sighed.

"I'll need you at my side Tim. Will you join me?"

He turned to face Tim and held out his hand. Tim looked at him so fixedly that John-Joe saw the tears start on his lower lids and creep onto his cheeks in spite of the rapid blinking. All the years of hero worship were in those tears. He dropped the conker, reached out and took John-Joe's hand in both of his. They shook hands silently until John-Joe loosened his grip. He turned away towards the Park gate, knowing that Tim would follow him, not to the gates of hell but to Dis, on its sixth level.

Later that night the lights were switched off in the *Danann* gym. The only illumination came from several small windows high against the lofty roof. Softly through the gloom, the glint of polished metal and the glow of white ropes defined the expanse and shape of the cavernous enclosed space. Some of the equipment cast faint shadows on the floor. One such was the globe cage in which John-Joe and Vinnie had battled. Across the *moire* pattern of the shadow of the mesh a darker shadow passed slowly. It was John-Joe, gripping the upper curves of the mesh with one hand and tucking his toes into the side curves as he crawled across the globe, his hurley gripped in the other hand. With silent and total concentration, he arched his body and reached as far towards the other side as he could with his hurley and hung there, motionless, his muscles quivering. It was the last day he would have access to the premises and the apparatus that allowed such concentrated muscular tension. This was his last change to absorb the formidable training environment that Curran had created in the service of his New Style Hurling. His letter of resignation, probably expected, was on Curran's desk and would be opened in the morning. It was the second resignation in as many weeks and he wondered at how fast events were moving for him whose life until now had been so ordered and predictable. This cage epitomised the highly-focused training which the style demanded of its practitioners and he, John-Joe, had absorbed the lessons and the techniques he had been exposed to over the past few months. Now he had to create a similar environment for his Kerry team but one in which there was room for skill, amidst the Neanderthal brutality of the *Danann*.

Suddenly the door to the offices opened and a bright shaft of light materialised across the polished floor. The shadows of two men broke into the shaft in long antlers of darkness.

"I told you to destroy it," it was Curran who spoke, softly and circumspectly.

"I decided to have it checked before I did. To see if you could tell whether it had been copied," it was O'Shea, also speaking softly.

The shadows stopped suddenly and Curran's voice crackled with anger.

"You showed it to someone!"

"Only parts of it. Parts that didn't make sense. Anyway, I found a technician who wasn't interested in the image, he was interested in what called the megadata embedded as the recording was made."

The shadows moved on and the two men came into John-Joe's line of vision. He breathed through open mouth for the sake of silence and willed his muscles to adapt to the strain and the required degree of silence.

"And what is that?" asked Curran.

"It's the way every camera marks a recording, automatically, behind the visual. It records the type of camera used, the shutter speed, the aperture, the GPS co-ordinates—"

"What use is that to us?"

"— and the time and date of the recording."

"All right, so?—"

"There was no megadata. It was removed. When the card was copied."

The figures stopped, next to the cage Jesus," said Curran. "That bastard. Where could he have put the original?"

"I know where he lived. I've had the place watched. Crosby lives there now, or did. Maybe we could ask him."

"No," Curran strode back and forth and stopped directly under John-Joe. "Who else lives there?"

"His sister, his mother, a lodger."

A drop of sweat fell from John-Joe's forehead and he watched it in horror as it fell clean through the mesh and onto Curran's shoulder.

"Search the place. Make it look like a burglary. I want no connection."

A soft pounding came from the large door at the back of the gym that lead into the service alley.

"Let him in. I think we should put the wind up our political friend."

As they moved towards the door, John-Joe's feet slipped and he hung suspended by one hand, his muscles screaming in agony. O'Shea punched a code into the keypad. He and Curran pushed the door partly open and another shaft of light, duller this time, bisected the one from the offices. A figure darted through.

"I'm not used to slingeing in by back alleys," said the man.

"And I'm not used to having my affairs known by someone who is so careless of possible consequences, Dougherty," replied Curran.

“Aah. You worry too much,” said Dougherty.

“I worry… appropriately,” said Curran. “I have just discovered that there is an existing videotape of our last meeting.”

“Shit! You told me you got that from Ring before you killed him—”

“We did. Unfortunately, it’s a copy. The original is out there, somewhere.”

“What are you going to do about it?”

“We’ll find it.” This was O’Shea.

“You better. Now where’s my money? I have to see certain people before the hearing.”

John-Joe, dangling from the mesh, saw a package change hands.

“The sum we agreed upon,” said Curran. “Make sure that Arena21 is… exonerated. I want this to be the last of the fucking hearings.”

Dougherty slipped out through the door and the other two pushed it closed. John-Joe took the opportunity to drop to the bottom of the cage. As the door rumbled on its tracks, he lowered the gate of the cage and dropped to the ground. Unsteadily, he ran for the office door. As he passed through, the hurley dropped from his sweating hand and clattered to the floor. The two men whirled and ran for the door. O’Shea stepped through the gap and looked to either side. Curran stooped and picked up the hurley. He turned it in his hands until the engraved name caught the light.

“Crosby,” he said.

Inside the headquarters office block, John-Joe ran as fast as he could to the reception area and then slowed down, controlling his heavy breathing. He stepped into the area, nodding to the security guard he knew would be on duty there.

“Stepping outside for a bit,” he said and passed out through the door, which the surprised guard activated for him. The guard knew him but was obviously puzzled as to why he would go out while wearing the *Danann* training outfit. Outside the door, John-Joe moved to the top of the steps and descended them. When he knew he was out of the guard's line of vision, he took a deep breath and ran down the dark street as fast as he could. He reached the corner before he heard the shouts and the clatter of footsteps behind him.

He was under no illusion as to the resources Curran could command and the speed at which he could deploy them. He had very little time to get away from the vicinity of the *Danann* headquarters before he was picked up by the security forces which numbered in the three figures, all readily activated and well supplied with cars and motorcycles. Sure enough, he was only metres from the corner when he heard the sound of cars accelerating behind him. He just had time to dodge off the main street into a smaller one when the headlights of a car swept the wall and a car roared past. He heard the sound of screeching brakes and a car reversing back towards the turnoff and he increased his already considerable speed.

He came out onto the street bordering the canal and hurtled down the grassy slope above the lock. It took him about four seconds to get onto the lock gate and lower himself down the slimy side and onto one of the massive cross beams but it was barely enough. The car stopped, the door opened and a figure wielding a bright torch ran onto the gate. Moving rapidly to the centre, the figure stopped and the beam of the torch swept around the lock and across to the far side, probing along the banks and around the base of the lime trees that lined the still, silvery strip of water.

He heard a muffled conversation on a mobile phone and seconds later another car approached on the far side of the canal. After a brief consultation, one car moved westwards along the bank and the other eastward, the passenger from each walking along the edge of the water, plying his torch. The beam of one of the torches swept across the surface of the water within the lock chamber, coming within a hand's breadth of his feet and then darted away, over the other gate and down the canal. John-Joe relaxed and very nearly lost his footing on the narrow beam but recovered and started his careful ascent.

When he emerged from the lock, he lifted his head slowly and surveyed the scene all round. The two cars and the attendant figures were moving away from him and the area was clear. Crawling across the grass onto the road, he looked carefully up and down the road before crossing, bent double. He reached the far side and moved swiftly up the side street and into the narrow streets that lay behind the houses along the canal banks. As he moved carefully through the dark, he pondered on what he should do. The Ring house in Stoneybatter was out of the question. That left Tim. It was Friday night and there would be a match in the Phoenix Park in the morning. So the Phoenix Park it was. Shivering, he headed in that general direction, breaking into a steady lope as he moved out of the danger zone.

17

The Phoenix Park was eerie at night. Gone was the sense of enclosure that the park had in the daytime, with its varied but limited vistas. In the monochrome gloom, the grass stretched into darkness to a distance impossible to estimate. The trees loomed in unfriendly bulk, their undersides dark and forbidding, their upper branches cold and distant. The enclosed plantations were the most sinister of all with their dense canopies and impenetrable murk. The open woodlands of larger trees were not much friendlier, with the whisper of wind amongst the branches and the movements of indeterminate animals among the boles. Above them the ragged clouds moved in streaks across the three-quarter moon. It was among these trees that John-Joe settled down to await the daylight and a long, cold night it proved to be.

Autumn was approaching and so he gathered up fallen leaves which were fortunately quite dry and made a bed of sorts under a particularly large chestnut tree. Lying down on some of the leaves and pulling the rest over him, he soon began to retain some of his body heat but as soon as he thought he had beaten one source of discomfort, another started. Ants or some such insects were attracted to his warmth, crawling under his clothing and exploring his ears, mouth and nostrils. He knew if he started scratching he would get no rest so, pulling the neck of his outfit up around his mouth and nose, he settled down to try to get some sleep.

Then the night noises started; the rustle of small animals or large insects, the munching sounds of some larger herbivore and the slithering sound of other creatures, perhaps foxes or hedgehogs as they moved across and through the leaves. Now and then came the hoot of an owl, the churr of a nightjar and the whirr of what sounded like bats off on their nightly hunt. This thought triggered off a rumbling in John-Joe's stomach and an almost overpowering feeling of emptiness. Closing his mind to these pangs, he eventually slept but fitfully.

Dawn, cold and grey, brought little relief. He came to his senses, stiff and hungry and in a state of disbelief. He was being hunted and he was lying, lightly dressed, in a pile of leaves, in a wood, in the middle of a large city. He had no money, no change of clothing and nowhere to go. His only chance was to make his way to the changing room in the Fifteen Acres, where Tim's team played and wait for Tim to arrive.

Throwing the leaves off, he got to his feet and brushed himself down as best he could. As he walked through the wood towards the Fifteen Acres, a dark shape moved from behind a tree and confronted him. It was a large black stag with enormous antlers. They stood and looked at each other for several long moments before the stag turned slowly away and back into the sheltering wood. He strode on across the grass until he came across a pond surrounded by trees. Crouching at the edge, he splashed some water on his face and hair and rubbed his hands in the cold, nearly stagnant liquid. It wakened both him and his hunger pangs and, his stomach protesting, he made his way towards the enormous cross which towered above the playing fields, commemorating the only pope who had ever visited Catholic Ireland.

As he reached the open spaces the Dublin hills became visible, low on the horizon. 'Mountains', the Dubliners called them and none of them higher that a Kerry foothill. Entering the changing room, he lay on the bench inside to wait, mulling over the options open to him. He persuaded himself that, when he heard what he knew about Tomas, Tim would bring him and Kitty together, somewhere Curran wouldn't find them and they would jointly work out a plan to use the information to best advantage.

Going to Kerry seemed a good option. He could make contact with Uncle Joe and help him get the Kerry team up to scratch for their match with the *Danann*. Immersed in these thoughts, the time passed and he heard the fields around coming to life as players approached and started to warm up. He sat up as footsteps approached the open door of the changing room. Two players entered and he remembered from the matches he had played with them. They stopped when they recognised him and his outfit and looked embarrassed.

"Is Tim here yet?" John-Joe asked.

"Yeah. He's outside with the other captain."

"Ask him to come in. And don't tell him I'm here. Please?"

They exchanged glances and left. Moments later Tim stood in the doorway.

"What are you doing here?" Tim asked.

"Is everything all right at home?"

"I don't know. I stayed over with… a friend last night. I haven't been home."

"You have a mobile?'

"Yes. What's all this—"

"Find out if everything's all right. Please?"

The earnestness of the last, almost shouted word persuaded Tim to take his phone out and dial. He listened, his eyes on John-Joe who paced up and down. Suddenly his jaw dropped open. John-Joe saw this and stepped up to him, looking anxiously into his face. Tim took the phone away from his ear, a distraught expression on his face.

"What!" John-Joe almost screamed.

"Mrs Ring," said Tim wonderingly.

"What about her?"

"She sounds… as if she's in shock. She just said 'Kitty. They took her. Kitty. Kitty'"

"Aw, Jesus."

"What's going on?"

"We've got to get there. Fast. But we mustn't be seen."

"What's happening?'

"Kitty's been kidnapped."

"By whom?"

"Curran. He killed Tomas. I heard him say so. Let's go. I'll tell you on the way. Anybody here got a car?"

"No. Fred's got a bike."

"It'll do."

John-Joe ran out onto the field. A heavy old upright bike was propped against the side of the hut. He grabbed it as Tim called out.

"Fred. We need your bike. Sorry fellas. Trouble. Big trouble."

He ran after John-Joe who was running with the bike to one of the minor roads. He called out over his shoulder.

"What's the quickest way? A way we can't be seen?"

"I'll ride. You get on the carrier. We'll head down to the small gate near the river and then go through the back streets around Arbour Hill."

Tim took the bike and mounted it and John-Joe climbed onto the metal carrier at the back. There was nowhere to put his legs, so he spread them out so they wouldn't drag on the ground. Tim stood on the pedals to get started and by dint of straining, managed to get the bike up to a respectable speed. He headed towards the hill down to the lower road and John-Joe, ignoring the pain in his buttocks from the metal and the insides of his thighs from the strain, explained what had happened the previous night. They reached the hill and picked up speed. Tim had some breath then to swear and rant at Curran. They came to one of the pedestrian gates in the park wall and manoeuvred the bike through. On the outside, they crossed the road before mounting and heading into the maze of narrow, quiet streets, on the way to Oxmantown Road.

"We must make sure Kitty is safe. If they have kidnapped her, we'll have to free her and then head for Kerry."

"Kerry?"

"Yes. I'll help Uncle Joe get the Kerry boys up to scratch, although I don't know yet how the hell they can get up to the same level as the *Danann*. You have no idea what the training involves."

"I do. I saw them in action. Here we are. The Ring house is beyond those houses. That house there backs onto their yard. Let's try to get through it."

They stopped outside one of the houses and Tim propped the bike against the wall as John-Joe knocked on the door. After a few seconds, the door opened part of the way and a thin, pinched, old male face filled the gap.

"What d'yiz want?" it asked suspiciously.

"We're at the house behind you and we've lost our key."

"What house?"

"Mrs Ring's house in—"

"I know no Mrs Ring."

"She lives in Oxmantown Road."

"Then why should I know her? I only know the people in this road."

"No reason you should but—"

The face had been looking at the very dirty and dishevelled training outfit worn by John-Joe."

"Hey. Isn't them the *Danann* colours?"

"Yes. We… we've been training and—"

"I like the *Danann*."

"Good. So you'll—"

I think yiz'll liven things up in hurling. Them bollixes in Kerry didn't deserve to win the All-Ireland."

"Well—"

"The *Danann*'ll kick the shite out of them, so they will."

"Well—"

"And them Kerry bollixes is so full of shite that it'll shower shite for days after the match."

"Well—"

"In fact, the gutters a Dublin will be running with Kerry shite for weeks after the *Danann* are finished with them."

"I suppose—"

"They're all bollixes."

"Can we—"

"They're even worse than them Offaly bollixes."

"Can we come in?"

"The country's full a bollixes."

"Yes," said John-Joe, meaning it. "It is."

"What do yiz want again?"

"To come through your house and into Mrs Ring's."

"Only if you promise to kick the shite outa them Kerry bollixes."

"I promise."

The face nodded in satisfaction turned abruptly away, leaving the door ajar. John-Joe and Tim ran down the hall, through the kitchen and out into the yard. The house felt damp and smelled of cabbage and urine. They left the face muttering 'Bollixes' in the kitchen and scaled the wall into the Ring's house.

18

When John-Joe tried to turn the handle on the back door of the Ring's house, it twisted loosely in his hand. It had been forced open and the mechanism broken. The kitchen was a shambles. Broken crockery, food and furniture lay in messy disorder on the floor. The hall door was open as was the door to the front room. His heart in his mouth, John-Joe entered the room, Tim on his heels. Mrs Ring was lying across the bed, gazing vacantly at the ceiling. The two men rushed to her and Tim took both her hands in his.

"Mrs Ring? Mrs Ring? It's Tim."

John-Joe laid his hand on Tim's shoulder and indicated the stairs. Tim nodded and turned back to Mrs Ring who had moved her stare onto his face.

"Mrs Ring. Can you tell me what happened?"

John-Joe ran up the stairs and looked into the two rooms and the bathrooms. He wasn't sure whether he was relieved or frightened that Kitty wasn't there because the room, floors and ceilings, had been ransacked. Almost all the electronic equipment was gone from his room and it looked as if a particularly resentful elephant had been through it. Not only were his possessions thrown on the floor, they had been deliberately destroyed, suits and shirts torn, linen shredded, shoes smashed. It was unbelievable, as if whoever had done it hated the owner of the goods and wanted to upset him as much as possible. The plasterboard from the ceiling was strewn about and the dusty rafters that hadn't see the light for a hundred years gaped idiotically.

He took the *Danann* suit off and donned an old sweater and pants of Tim's and went downstairs again. In the kitchen the cupboard which had held, amongst other things, the liquor, was upright, its doors sagging limply on their hinges. He peered into the dark interior and there in the corner was the small bottle he had presented to Mrs Ring on his arrival at the house. He took it up and shook it. There was at least one measure of poteen left in it. He took it and looked for a glass. None had survived the rampage but an unbroken cup lay against the wall. He took it up, rinsed it under the tap and poured the contents in.

Back in the front room. Mrs Ring was looking at Tim blankly. John-Joe, nudged Tim and offered the cup. Tim sniffed it and smiled grimly. John-Joe slipped his arms under Mrs Ring and lifted her gently into a sitting position. Tim held the cup against her lips and waited. The fumes from the poteen stimulated some reflex in her. Her lips reached out and Tim tilted the cup so that some liquid could flow into her mouth. She swallowed and sighed and her eyes came slowly into focus. She looked at Tim and muttered; "Kitty."

"Where's Kitty?"

There was no answer.

"Did someone take her?"

Mrs Ring nodded slowly.

"Was she hurt?"

Mrs Ring shook her head and reached her mouth towards the cup again. Tim applied the last of the poteen.

"Kitty," said Mrs Ring again.

"What'll we do with her?" asked Tim.

"Get her to Kerry. To Uncle Joe."

"How?"

"Don't they have taxis in Dublin?"

Tim helped settle Mrs Ring back onto the bed and reached for his mobile.

It took an hour to get Mrs Ring settled into a taxi and the driver paid the fare to Kerry, where he would receive a bonus payment if he got his passenger to Joe Crosby's house in one piece. This had been arranged by John-Joe on the phone to Joe, after he had explained in brief outline what had happened.

Then the two of them set out to hire a car and drive to the *Danann* headquarters.

John-Joe had got his first whiff of fear on the sea cliffs of Kerry. Near Cahirciveen, on the famed Ring of Kerry scenic route, an older cousin had taken him down the cliff to where vast colonies of nestless guillemots perched, to purloin the pear-shaped eggs from the ledges. Without the aid of a rope he followed his cousin down the rugged cliff face, feeling such confidence in his reckless relative that he hadn't the inclination to be scared.

That was until they reached the swarming mass of birds, which were jostling each other for space, the eggs clutched between their legs. As they rested before taking the eggs, John-Joe looked out over Dingle Bay to where the Blasket Islands lay, surf-rimmed in the dark Atlantic. Then he looked down and his muscles froze and the breath left his lungs. The rocks plunged for a million miles beneath the ledge on which they sat. The sound of the surf, which he knew was tremendous, was drowned both by the growling of thousands of guillemots and the pounding of blood in his ears.

"Come on," said his cousin, standing up prior to climbing further down to where the shoulder-to-shoulder tumult began.

"Don't," said John-Joe weakly, the blood pounding faster.

"Don't what? Oh. The height's got you? Never mind. It happens to everybody. Let's sit here until it goes away."

And they sat there for several minutes until John-Joe's blood stopped pounding through his veins and the sweat dried up and the sickening feeling in his stomach went away. Strangely enough, when all these enervating symptoms disappeared, a feeling of extreme wellbeing took their place.

"Come on," he said, getting to his feet and moving towards the birds. His cousin laughed loudly.

"It's always the same. After you stop being shit scared you become shit careless. Don't get too confident. It's a long way down."

Laughing loudly, John-Joe yelled at the birds and started loading the eggs down inside the open neck of his shirt. From then on, scaling the cliffs for the eggs of guillemots, kittiwakes, gannets and fulmars became a favourite pastime and boiling the eggs in an old tin can over a fire of dried seaweed became a post-climbing ritual.

So, scaling up and across the vast external sidewall of the *Danann* gym, up to where the small, high windows let in the light was no big deal, even in the dark. Opening the windows, which were always left slightly ajar, was also no problem. As he did so, he saw a pool of light far down the gym. Caught in it, pinioned to the climbing bars by a thick, white gym rope was Kitty. She was spreadeagled and almost naked, the ropes wrapped around her outstretched arms and legs. In the gloom in front of her stood a man, tapping a ball up and down on a hurley. John-Joe slipped silently through the window and swung onto one of the large, exposed beams of wood which, braced as they were on the walls, supported the roof. One of the beams passed quite near to a rope suspended from rings high on the wall. That would be his route to the ground. As he started his descent, the man spoke. It was Vinnie.

"I am going to hurt you and fuck you and hurt you and fuck you until you tell me where that tape is," he said. "You won't scratch me again because your arms will be broken."

John-Joe stopped immobilised by rage. He looked down to see Vinnie wipe his hand across his face, spit and then send the ball straight at Kitty. It passed close to her elbow and Kitty let out a little scream. John-Joe recovered and resumed climbing, gritting his teeth as he heard Vinnie speak again.

"Your legs will be broken too. And that will make fucking you very interesting."

Another thud and another stifled scream. Tap, tap, tap went the ball.

"Years ago, I went to a circus. There was this knife thrower," said Vinnie as he hit another ball. There was no scream this time. "This bird was tied to a wall. Jaysus. Those knives went close. As close as *that*." There was another thud and the ball went bouncing back into the gloom behind Vinnie. John-Joe was now on the ground and he waited for the next exertion by Vinnie to mask his movement towards them.

"Then he did it blindfold. I wonder how that felt. Let's find out."

Vinnie hit another ball and this time it connected with Kitty's hip. She gasped in agony, her breath taken away by the pain.

"Oh, sorry. Let's try that again," said Vinnie, reaching with his hurley to flick up another ball. As he stooped down, the ball thrown by John-Joe with all his strength, caught him on the first and second cervical vertebrae, where the spinal column joins the skull. The shock to the spinal cord was traumatic. It spread into all parts of Vinnie's brain and his consciousness closed down. He dropped senseless to the floor.

John-Joe appeared out of the gloom and ran to Kitty, the thick rope was quickly and easily loosed and he caught Kitty in his arms as she slumped free. He gathered her up and ran towards the back door of the gym.

"Bastards!" sobbed Kitty, her voice shuddering with the running motion. "You're all bastards. The whole hurling, pucking, fucking lot of you."

"Come on Kitty. Let's get you to Kerry."

19

"There are Kerry men here and men from Tip and West Cork. There's even a man from Offaly."

On a stretch of mountain pasture, on Beginish, one of the lonely Blasket Islands, a motley crew of brawny men were lined up in training gear. Joe Crosby was walking along the line, glaring into each face. Beginish was the Island closest to the Kerry shore. It was isolated, the last inhabitants having been two brothers who left in the 1990s. Quirk had isolated it further by arranging the cancellation of the few cruises for holidaymakers which were organised by the local fishermen on the mainland. He had brought in some high-speed boats, two helicopters and several armed drones to take care of any aerial surveillance that might be organised by Curran or curious media houses.

John-Joe was watching them closely. Some he knew, some he had played with and some were strangers. He had to decide which of them would make a good team to bring up to the standards of the *Danann*. He had left Kitty at Uncle Joe's place, where Mrs Ring had installed herself and was running a household against which Joe Crosby chafed but secretly enjoyed being fussed over and having a hearty meal and warm slippers waiting for him every time he returned home.

"But you know what?" Joe continued. "You're a bunch of nobodies. A group of gobshites. You're not fit to face the ould women in the local sodality, never mind the *Danann*. Do you know what they'll do to you? Every mother's son of you? They'll reach down your gullet, grab your arsehole and pull you inside out like a sweaty sock. They'll take your *caman*, snap it across their perpetual erections and stick the smooth end up your back passage, so you get splinters in your hands pulling it out."

The men found it difficult to keep straight faces.

"Smile would you? By Jesus they'll knock them smiles of yours into the middle of next month. You've seen them in action. They're not men any more, they're killing machines. And you've got to beat them."

"Fortunately," Joe continued. "John-Joe has trained – and played – with them."

There was a growl from some of the men.

"He went there because I told him to. He's back here with their training methods and he's going to teach them to you, so you'll know what to expect."

He stepped back and John-Joe came forward with one of the *Danann* hurleys. He carried two balls.

"They all have these hurleys," he said, swishing it through the air in one of the Eastern manoeuvres he had been taught in the *Danann*. "Thady, you've the longest puck in Kerry. Show us now what you can do with your *caman*."

He tossed the ball to Thady who preened a bit and then pucked with an easy, liquid swing of his broad shoulders. The ball soared across the pasture and into the gorse. There were several murmurs of admiration. John-Joe stepped forward. He had their total attention. He threw the ball onto the grass, flicked it up in the air and swung his hurley at it as it was halfway down to the ground. The leather covering burst open and flapped to the ground. The inner core screamed out of sight. There was a stunned silence.

"That's just one advantage they have. Then there's the new ball."

He turned to Joe who took one of the *Danann* balls out of his pocket and lobbed it to John-Joe.

"This ball is specially designed to withstand the impact of such a *caman*. Feel it. It's like a cannonball."

He threw it hard at one of the men who caught it in mid-air and winced at the impact. The men passed it to and fro as John-Joe continued.

"The other advantages? Well I'll do my best to teach them to you but it's going to be hard. You're going to do a lot of swearing, mostly at me. You're going to get angry – at each other. You're going to turn that anger into aggression. Controlled aggression. Deadly aggression. You're going to make the elimination of each and every *Danann* your personal mission. Your total focus."

They looked at him as if he was mad and he felt a sinking feeling. They were strong and tough and in prime physical condition but there was no ruthlessness in them. Each of them was capable of playing dirty but the degree of lethal mayhem of which every *Danann* was capable was beyond their comprehension, perhaps beyond their capabilities. He turned to Joe and they started a warm-up routine.

An old barn on the island had been converted into a gym with most of the required equipment donated by Quirk from a list supplied by John-Joe and several prefabricated buildings had been erected around the perimeter, serving as offices. He and Joe had divided the training routines between them. Joe concentrated on honing the men's normal hurling skills. John-Joe's task was to imbue them with as much of the eastern martial arts techniques and the cold, unemotional frame of mind which the *Danann* regime developed but he was groping and making it up as he went along. He realised that while he knew exactly the outcome he wanted, he had no idea how to instill the requisite attitudes in the men. Quirk had thrown himself wholeheartedly into the project, with time, energy and money. He had a science laboratory in Johannesburg working on reproducing the lethal hurley and balls of the *Danann.* A sports outfitter in Boston was manufacturing all the requisite clothing, footwear and protective gear. The designs, patterns and specifications for all of these were available on the *Danann* website for a licensing fee which John-Joe thought modest until he calculated the sheer volume of fees as manufacturers all over the world catered for the ever-increasing demand generated by the blossoming number of new-style-hurling clubs springing up everywhere. Some of the clothing had become street style amongst teenagers, especially the black and Hispanic sectors in the USA. This swelled the demand and the revenue to Curran's organisation. Quirk has organised the setting up of a tented village for the team and the support staff. The accommodation was sparse but comfortable and the isolation afforded by the Island was conducive to the high level of concentration that John-Joe and Joe demanded from everybody. Quirk, again, had laid on daily helicopter shuttles between the island and an airport close to Tralee. Quirk had also persuaded Bull O'Connor to come down to regulate the dietary routine of the team and to devise a series of body-building exercises. It was all highly effective and the men responded with a will. Joe was delighted with their progress and John-Joe had to mask his own feelings of discouragement so as not to deflate his uncle.

"They're the best crowd of men I've ever had," Joe said proudly, three weeks into the training period. He, Quirk and John-Joe were watching the men at their exercises. "Look at them. They're swelling visibly."

"Are they up to the *Danann* yet?" asked Quirk.

"Not yet," replied John-Joe and quickly spoke as he saw Joe's face fall. "But we'll get there."

"Well, I've got a surprise for you," said Quirk. "I liked your idea of creating different sort of mental and physical approach to the *Danann*. An alternative philosophy as it were, one that you are not equipped to devise or to implement. So I found somebody for you."

He turned and headed for one of the prefabs and the others followed. Inside they were surprised to see, sitting on a long bench, a small, thin oriental man with long white hair and a wispy beard that hung down to his chest. On a bench behind him sat two oriental men with expressionless faces who kept their eyes on the floor. The man stared at John-Joe, paying no attention as Quirk introduced him simply as Mr Li. Li spoke to John-Joe as if the other two weren't present. His voice was soft, accent-less and precise.

"You are the young man who is confronting the *Danann* team? Well, I have watched them in operation and I see no reason why you should not overcome their rather... crude... tactics. Sit please."

The others sat on the bench facing Li.

"You have not a lot of time but it should be sufficient. I will need to work with seven of your team and two of your reserves, if they become necessary. They will comprise you as the Centre Half Back and whoever you choose as the Centre Forward, Left and Right Half Forwards, and Left and Right Half Backs, with the person you most depend on, on your strongest side. Also the Full Back. I will take you and them in hand. The rest will continue with normal training. Their purpose will be to supply raw and brutal power to create space for the chosen seven to operate according to my instructions and training. Is that clear?"

"Yes," said John-Joe, surprised at the man's grasp of the sport. "However, there is one person on the *Danann* who—"

"Vinnie. Yes," replied Li. "He will play Centre Forward if I'm not mistaken." John-Joe nodded. "It is the position of power and of arrogance. Both will be his weakest points. Bring the chosen players here tomorrow morning."

He lapsed into silence and the others left the building. Outside Quirk spoke.

"The other players, the… battering rams. Are they good enough?"

"They're good," said Joe. "The best I've ever handled."

"But?"

"They're not… tough enough," said John-Joe. "And I don't know if they ever will be frankly."

"That's all right so," said Quirk. "If it's toughness you want. I'll get you tough."

"We're talking about real toughness," said John-Joe.

"So am I," replied Quirk, turning to go.

"Where will you get tough—"

Quirk spun back and leaned over John-Joe and spoke in a hard, low whisper.

"You don't know – and you never will – want to know the answer to that question, lad."

20

The Blasket Islands, especially Begenish had always meant a great deal to Kitty. She and Tomas used to go out there on the ferry from Dunquin on the mainland and explore the coastline with its towering cliffs and occasional isolated beaches until it was time to catch the ferry back.

When she left the fast-recovering Mrs Ring in Joe's house and came to the Island, she suggested doing the same with John-Joe later that morning after the meeting with Li, he had agreed with alacrity and off they went on one of the three remaining boats. The weather was fine, a few cirrus clouds high up promised wind later on but in the early morning, the air was still and the surf subdued. Half an hour cruising from the tiny harbour brought them around the craggy headland and the silvery sand of a beach came into view. The cliffs stood up proud at one side of the sandy stretch but on the other side, the land rose in gentle swells up a virtual valley until it reached the same height as the cliff tops.

"There it is. I remember it well."

The keel of the craft ground on the sand and John-Joe leapt out and pulled it half out of the water. Kitty jumped down lightly onto the sand, carrying the basket into which she had packed a light lunch. High up on one cliff face, the guillemots perched, swooped and fought for space on the ledges.

"Fancy a guillemot egg or two?" he asked her.

"I don't know if I could eat one now," she said.

"I bet you could. Get a fire going."

He ran to the cliff and started to climb while she gathered some dried seaweed and made a small pile of it. She took a can of cola out of the basket and opened it. She watched John-Joe climb as she sipped the chill drink. He reminded her so much of Tomas, the same impetuousness and lack of fear but with a more level-headed streak in him than Tomas ever had. He was near the birds now and he turned to look down and wave at her. She returned the wave and then, twisting some paper napkins from the basket into wisps, tucked them in among the seaweed and lit them. The fire took quickly so she finished the cola and, using the combined corkscrew/tin opener from the basket, she took the top off the can, filled it with sea water and perched it on two small stones among the burning weed to boil.

By this time John-Joe was down with several eggs tucked into his shirt. He dropped them gently into the water which was boiling and they settled down to wait. The day was getting hotter so he stripped off his shirt and enjoyed the warmth on his skin. She was surprised at how much his musculature had developed since she had last seen him naked. Leaning over, she ran her fingers across his shoulder and down his bicep.

"The *Danann* training made a new man of you," she said softly.

He laughed and flexed the muscles of his arm.

"Man of steel," he said and then looked soberly at her. "Back there… in the gym… did… did Vinnie…"

"Have his way with me? No. These took his mind off… other things."

She dragged her fingernails down his chest and across his nipple. He shivered slightly and leaned towards her.

"The eggs," she said.

He took a clasp knife out of his pocket and scooped out the eggs onto the sand. Wrapping a paper napkin around one, he sliced the top off one and offered it to her. Gingerly she scooped some of the yolk out with her finger and popped it into her mouth. She mushed it slowly around her mouth with her tongue, considering.

"Not bad. Not as good as I remember."

"It never is, is it?" he replied as he scooped some into his mouth. "Ah. Now *that's* a taste!"

"You've got some on your chin," she said, leaning into him and licking the egg off. Their mouths met in a long, investigatory kiss. When they finished they drew apart and looked at each other. She pushed him back onto the sand and stroked his chest and hard, flat stomach. Her hands brushed across the belt of his trousers and down to where his erection was pushing the cloth away from his groin. She caressed it, enjoying the increasing bulk, then she moved back to his belt and undid it. He lifted his hips as she pushed his trousers and underpants down. Exposed, his penis grew to its full extent, triumphant in the sun. She bent down and took it in her mouth and he sighed deeply with pleasure as her lips moved up and down slowly. After a few delicious moments, she rolled away, whisked off her skirt and pants and rolled back to sit astride him, her hot, wet vagina pressing down on the shaft of his penis. He groaned as she reached back and undid her bra and her full breasts dangled in front of him. Reaching up he took one of her erect nipples in his mouth and she threw her head back and laughed softly.

Then she froze.

"The cottage," she said.

"No," he said hoarsely, trying to manoeuvre his penis into her. "It's fine here!"

But she was off him looking up the valley.

"The cottage. It's the cottage in the video."

She grabbed her clothing and dressed hurriedly. He rolled over onto his knees and looked down despairingly at his penis, fast assuming its normal flaccid state. He grabbed it and groaned.

"Leave yourself alone," she said. "Come on."

He rearranged his clothing and, going down to the water, splashed some on his face and groin. Then he followed her towards the cottage. She was right. It was the roofless cottage in Tomas's video, in the same rugged glen, with the same distinctively-shaped hilltop over it. They approached it carefully and walked in through where the door used to hang.

"Look," Kitty said.

There was a small, robust tin box in the fireplace, lying on its side.

"Looks like it fell down," John-Joe said. "It must have been on a ledge in the chimney."

He took up the box and undid the clasp. Inside was a sealed static-proof envelope. Inside that was a video card wrapped in several layers of tinfoil. Kitty took it up and held it to her breast.

"There'll be a player for that in Tralee," said John-Joe.

21

John-Joe had sent Kitty to the mainland on the army helicopter and was busy working on the men when the chopper returned and landed in a cloud of grit and sand next to Joe's cottage. Out of the craft jumped six of the toughest looking men John-Joe had ever seen. They looked like character actors from Central Casting and each carried a large tog bag. Quirk emerged from the helicopter last. He moved over to where Joe and John-Joe were standing.

"These men will do anything," said Quirk, after a perfunctory greeting. "Just teach them the rudiments of the game, so they blend in."

He nodded at one of the men who reached into his tog bag and pulled out a hurley. Quirk took it and passed it to John-Joe.

"Exactly like the *Danann*'s," said Quirk. "except for these little details." He indicated some angled protuberances above the holding end of the *caman* and a rounded lip at the very end. "They were Li's idea and the GAA has given their approval. Should even up the odds a bit. They're all yours."

He started back towards the helicopter which took off immediately.

John-Joe looked after it for a moment before returning to the six strange men.

"All right," he said. "Let's see if we can make you blend in."

He handed them over to Joe and headed for the prefab to meet Li who was sitting on a bench with an acolyte behind him. As soon as John-Joe entered, Li held out his hand and his acolytes placed a new hurley in it. Li held it in both his hands and addressed John-Joe.

"Mine is the old discipline, when judo – the gentle art – was the lodestone of all Japanese martial arts. The objective was to learn rather than to compete and it was based on using the other's momentum to achieve victory. Resistance to a powerful other will invariably result in defeat. But adjusting to his attack will destroy his balance and reduce his power. I have adapted your hurley to help you achieve that. The *Danann* are trained to use it as an attacking weapon. This addition," he indicated the small protuberance at the front of the holding end "will help deflect the other's attacking stroke by deflecting it – and the power of the stroke – away from the hand. This," he indicated the protuberance at the very end of the hurley, "allows you to reverse the stick." He reversed the hurley and made a chopping motion with it. "Turning it into an effective axe to be used to dislodge the hurley from the other's grip as he passes, thus disarming him. You will practise this move until it becomes second nature. The fencing foil, the most elegant of weapons, relies on the deflection and the diffusion of force to conquer and can keep the heavier epee or even the sabre at bay for the fatal thrust to the body. Do I make myself clear?"

He handed the hurley to John-Joe who took it and twirled it in his hand until the sharp edge of toe faced outwards and swung it in an arc.

"You see? Your conditioning and your present state of mind, instinctively seeks the weapon in the stick. You must rid yourself of these attitudes. By concentrating the force focused on a sharp and small part of the stick, you are entering the *Danann* frame of reference and indeed the frame of references of most modern martial arts. These appeal to the baser instincts of the participants and the audiences and are to be avoided at all costs. The skill and training required to move away from this brutality will give you space in which to demonstrate the grace and subtleties of the game. Which I assume is your overall objective."

"Yes. Undoubtedly," replied John-Joe.

"Well keep that in the forefront of your mind and instill it into the players. All except Mr Quirk's men. They are personifications of brute force but even they will be used for diffusion and deflection. If you adopt the Garryowen manoeuvre from rugby, which I suggest you should, those men will be the living wedge following the ball driven before them and their job is to push the *Danann* aside to provide one or two of your key players access to their goal. Think of the reed which bends with the great flood and survives when the strong and powerful tree breaks. Think of the open palm and how it can master the closed fist."

John-Joe's mind was reeling with a form of data overload but he forced himself to concentrate. This was just as well because Li was far from finished.

"We have schools of Shaolin monks in Japan. Perhaps you have heard of them?"

"Yes. In fact, I went to one of their shows some time ago."

"Yes. A pity. Those shows exposed only the flashy, superficial aspect of their rigorous training. Their real skill is the increasing ability they are developing to overcome gravity, if only for a brief moment, they can focus the momentum of their fast-moving bodies on a near-vertical surface, balance it and neutralise the strong force that created the galaxies and destroys stars. Reflect on these things Mr Crosby until they supplant almost all you currently know about your sport. Then you can start to reformulate the classic hurling style and present it to a discerning audience. You and I will have these tutorials regularly and I will watch your training methods to satisfy myself that you are instilling them into the team."

Having sat alone on a rocky headland, watching the pounding surf of the Atlantic and turning over in his mind the demanding but very exciting philosophy which Li had exposed him to, John-Joe sought out Tim and explained the new focus. Tim became as excited as he was about the potential of resuscitating the classic style and the strong probability that they could beat the *Danann* by playing against their style. While Tim concentrated on starting to re-focus the minds of the existing players, John-Joe started with Quirk's men. These men, when they spoke at all, did so in strong Northern Ireland accents. Joe soon found out that there were immensely fit and tough as nails. They were also totally disciplined and accepted every aspect of the training regimen. At first the rest of the players kept them at arm's length and treated them very distantly but, with Joe bellowing and John-Joe and Tim cajoling equally at everybody, they soon accepted them as a vital part of the team. Indeed, it soon became clear that they would play a crucial role in the coming match. They all had been trained in unarmed combat which included many of the martial arts techniques resorted to by the *Danann*. They were also impervious to damage. Each of them could emerge from the most ferocious melee intact and not even breathing heavily. They withstood the most fearsome tackles and brushed off the many injuries they sustained before they got the hang of dodging hurleys in a tangle of men.

Using the hard men as shock troops, Joe and John-Joe developed the Garryowen manoeuvre and devised other tactics designed to get them close to the goal where their power could be unleashed with devastating effect. Another tactic was to use them as shields or flying wedges to clear a path for the accomplished hurlers to strategic positions from which they could score. It emerged that the new men were all trained in full-contact karate and this would save the bones of the other players, so they could launch an attack with full force and contain the energy nanoseconds before actual contact. It scared the other players at first but in the long run, gave them much more confidence and poise. The new men kept to themselves, in their own tents. They ate alone and rarely mixed socially. Not only were they material fit to face the *Danann* but they injected a streak of ferocity into the team which had been lacking. Within a week, John-Joe's confidence level had risen dramatically. With this calibre of men, he could give as good as he got, even from the *Danann*.

22

Kitty could only find one likely source of a compatible video player on which to view the card. It proclaimed itself as a TV repair shop but the contents weren't very reassuring to her when she entered. The place was packed with equipment which included lawnmowers, bicycles, kitchen implements – both electric and manual – radios, gramophones and just a few TV sets. All were in varying stages of decay and dismemberment.

The man behind the counter didn't inspire much confidence either. He was extraordinarily thin, with thick, dirty glasses, through which he peered at her, an idiotic grin on his face. He took the proffered video card in hands that boasted the filthiest fingernails she had ever seen and held it very close to his eyes.

"T'riffic technology this," he said. "4G high definition. Five to one compression. Two-channel *and* would you believe *four*-channel audio modes. Fuck – sorry – God knows how many gigabytes. Analogue's long dead, you know." He looked around his dusty stock and sighed. "So is tape. *Marbh*. Kafuckingput. Sorry again. And it has," he peered "ten – no I lie – fifteen micron track pitch. T'riffic."

He smirked at her in triumph.

"Can I view it?"

"Oh no. No. No. Not here you can't. You see that technology hasn't reached Tralee yet."

She took the card and left.

"But it's coming," he called after her. "Don't you worry."

He looked around the shop.

"T'riffic technology," he sighed.

Kitty's next port of call was Quirk's estate. She took a taxi there and was deposited at the gate. The security guard left his lodge, approached the gate and asked her what she wanted.

"Kitty Ring for Mr Quirk," she said.

"Kitty Ring for Mr Quirk," he repeated into his mobile and stood impassively, waiting for an answer. The answer came and he clicked off his phone, gestured to the taxi to depart and opened the gate for Kitty to enter.

"They'll fetch you," he said, locking the gate and re-entering his lodge.

It was two or three minutes before a black limousine came down the curved driveway and pulled up beside her. The back door opened and she got in. The door closed and the vehicle pulled away back up the drive.

The drive wound through stands of broad-leaved trees and around ornamental ponds before it drew up in front of an extensive baronial style house in dull grey ashlar stone, with a wide stairway leading up to a huge oaken door, which stood ajar. The sunshine lay dully on the castellations along the top of the building and glinted slyly on the many small windows. For all its bulk, it was a pinched, suspicious-looking house and Kitty could well imagine Quirk, whom she had never taken to and never quite trusted, living in it.

She got out of the car and made her way up the steps. As she approached the door a formidable muscle-bound man in a morning suit stepped out through the door.

"Please follow me, Miss Ring," he said and walked back in.

She did so and wasn't at all surprised to see the weaponry, flags and suits of armour distributed about the enormous hall. They crossed it and entered a smaller room on the far side. Quirk was waiting for her, standing in front of a bright log fire. He gave a slight bow and gestured for her to take a seat at a table in the enclosure of the bay window. She did so and cast a glance at the silvery river that wound along the side of the house before plunging into some dark woods. The table was set for tea. Without asking her he poured for both of them, speaking the meanwhile.

"A great hurling family, the Rings. I've followed their play for generations. Fine, fine players the lot of them. Sugar?"

"Two, thank you. The men, certainly."

He caught the note of impatience.

"But you didn't come here to talk about hurling, did you?" He passed her cup, thin, exquisite bone china, filled with very weak tea. Her worst.

"No. I… I need access to some very advanced video playback equipment."

"Which they don't have in Tralee."

"No."

"Can you describe the equipment?"

"No. I… I have a video recording."

"May I see it?"

Reluctantly she produced the card from her pocket. She made no move to hand it to him. He stared to reach for it but lowered his hand again and looked closely at the card.

"Ah. I'm afraid it's unlikely that can be played on the equipment I have here. May I ask what it contains?"

She said nothing.

"I understand your caution. I also understand the circumstances you – and John-Joe – find yourselves in." She still said nothing. "Vinnie Murphy. O'Shea. Curran." No reaction. "Tomas."

She looked at him in some shock.

"I've made it my business to look after John-Joe's well-being. I know the danger he – and you – are in. I have applied my not inconsiderable forces on his protection. May I extend that protection to you? You are in need of it with that."

"You know what's on it?" She was disbelieving.

"No. But I can surmise that it was recorded by your brother before he was killed." That roused her interest. "And that it contains something that someone, somewhere, doesn't want somebody else to see."

"Yes. That someone is Curran. It is evidence against him."

Quirk sat up a little straighter.

"And it is conclusive?"

"Tomas would not have been killed if it weren't."

"Ah," he sighed. "Then you need to get it to Dublin and into the hands of a man who is code named Setanta. He and I were… associated… for many years but now he affords the only access you can possibly have to genuine, uncompromised justice in this country. However, travelling to Dublin to view it wouldn't be wise. I have an associate in Galway whom you will be able to trust, once I have a word with him."

"What's the fastest way to Galway?"

He rang a little silver bell on the table.

23

Killaloe Harbour basked in the unaccustomed sunshine. Several cruisers bobbed at their moorings on the silvery water. Amongst them lurked an enormous, black steel barge with a stout wooden superstructure. Grey smoke rose from the chimney in the roof.

John-Joe walked along the pier, stepping over the many mooring lines until he drew level with the barge's name plate which read 'The Cold Eye'. He grinned in recognition and stepped towards the small gangplank. Into his line of vision came an incredibly hairy face, wrapped around two pale grey eyes. It protruded from a porthole in the side of the superstructure.

"Well?" the face asked. "Do you recognise the name?"

"*Cast a cold eye, on life, on death,*" said John-Joe. "*Horseman pass by.*"

"Good on you. Come aboard."

The face laughed and disappeared as John-Joe mounted the gangplank. When he reached the deck, the face appeared again on top of a brawny body clad in faded blue dungarees. A huge hand was offered to him and he placed his own hand into a warm, firm handshake.

"Anybody who recognises Yeats's epitaph is afforded a real welcome. Anyone else is tolerated. I'm McGarrity."

"I'm John-Joe Crosby."

"I guessed you were. You have the look of a hurler about you."

McGarrity led the way into the barge which was very comfortably fitted out in an open-plan style. The furniture and fittings in the one long cabin were clustered around the main domestic activities; eating, dining, relaxation and sleeping. Heavy curtains were drawn up against the bulwarks, ready to divide the sections more clearly. They were in the galley and a rich smell of roasting meat hung in the air.

"You're in time for lunch," said McGarrity. "Lamb. It's not often that I indulge in a roast but when I do, it tastes divine. A drop of wine?"

"Thank you."

McGarrity took a wine glass from an open dresser and half filled it with red wine from an open bottle on the table. He handed the glass to John-Joe and took up another glass which was half full.

"Gevrey-Chambertin," he said. "God's greatest gift to tipplers."

John-Joe sipped at the rich, heady liquid. It was superb and he conveyed his pleasure with a smile. McGarrity laughed and walked into the seating area. He gestured at the packed bookshelves that lined the wall.

"Wine and poetry. Every great vintage for the past twenty years and every first edition of Willie Yeats. Well, nearly every. There's a bastard in Washington who has the only autographed first edition of *The Tower* and he won't part with it."

John-Joe sat on the couch and sipped his wine. McGarrity laughed again and sipped his.

"I tried to buy his tower," he said.

"Yeats's tower?"

"Yes. Toor Ballylee. It's owned by Bord Failte and they've put a bloody theatre in there. Yeats would be furious."

"What would you have done with it?"

"Turned it into the greatest poetry-reading venue in the world."

"Wouldn't get a big crowd in that place."

"Crowd? Who said anything about a crowd? I would have gathered ten of the world's greatest poets and had them read to each other."

"You can do that anywhere."

"No. You need a tower for the right resonance. Carl Jung had one in Bollingen. So had Rainer Maria Rilke – *Turriphilia*. They all had one. I have a barge. Ah! Lunch should be just about ready. Come."

He walked to the stove and took out a leg of lamb. John-Joe's stomach reacted to the pungent smell. McGarrity took a formidable carving set out of a drawer and started to whet the knife.

"However," he said, the wide blade flashing. "You're not here to talk about poetry, are you?"

"No. Dennis Quirk said I should talk to you about our marketing."

McGarrity caught the slight dismissive nuance in John-Joe's tone.

"And you're not convinced that your team needs marketing, are you?"

"Well…"

McGarrity attacked the roast with a deft stab of the carving fork and smooth slashes of the knife. The juice of the perfectly roasted meat ran onto the carving board and the thin slices fell away in regular curves.

"Take those plates out, will you? Thanks. What effect does a partisan crowd have on the outcome of a match, would you say?"

"It can decide a match, one way or the other," said John-Joe, as McGarrity laid several meat slices along the sides of each of the plates.

"And what decides the attitude of each and every crowd?"

"The relative skills of the teams, or players."

McGarrity took a dish of roasted onions, aubergines, beans and potatoes out of the oven and dispensed them around the meat.

"Partly," he said.

"Partly?"

"While every crowd has its *aficionados*, seventy-five percent of any crowd watching any sport are unaware of the finer points of that game. They react to direct and simple movements of a ball or a player or whatever determines the fate of a game. Gravy?"

"Yes. Thank you."

On went a generous serving of rich, dark liquid.

"There. That'll stick to your ribs," said McGarrity as he took the plates and brought them to the table. "Bring the wine and help yourself to another glass."

John-Joe did as he was bid and they both sat and tackled the meal. It was one of the tastiest John-Joe had ever eaten and the wine complemented it to perfection. They ate for a while in reverent silence, nodding and smiling their appreciation.

"More?" asked McGarrity as the plates emptied.

"No. Any more would spoil the enjoyment."

They both eased back in their chairs and sipped the wine. After a moment. McGarrity spoke.

"The attitude which a crowd brings *to* a match is a product of the attitude created in its collective consciousness *before* a match."

"By marketing?"

"Yes. Nationalism plays a part of course. If it is a match between nations, the attitude has been formed over years. It taps into such deep, ingrained emotions as custom, territoriality, even historic wars. If it is a match between competing styles, or newly-formed entities such as the *Danann* and the Kerry team which you are busy re-inventing, that attitude has to be mobilised almost from scratch. And Curran has a lead on you. He has newness on his side and the word 'new' is so powerful that there are several laws in several countries forbidding its use in marketing unless the product is genuinely new. But his newness can be turned into his weakness with the right techniques. Coffee? I don't do sweets."

"Coffee's fine."

"Then we'll chug up as far as Loch Derg while I persuade you that not only will you benefit from some high-powered marketing, you'll almost certainly lose without it."

On deck, John-Joe stood behind McGarrity while he steered the boat along what he called 'the last un-fucked-up river in Europe.' McGarrity wasn't long in getting down to business.

"Now we've got to talk about the public attitudes, both in the minds of TV watchers and, more importantly to you, on the day, on the field. You know how the emotional backing of spectators can impact directly on the players and increase their performance?"

John-Joe had used such backing too often to disagree.

"Of course you do. You're the greatest hurler in Ireland so you know how to get a crowd on your side." Again, John-Joe nodded in agreement. "Well," continued McGarrity, "You must concentrate on making the *Danann* 'the other' while you position yourselves as the underdogs to begin with. The *Danann* newness – strangeness – helps make this 'otherness' and we all know how that feeling can undermine the deepest-rooted cores of human sympathy in the human race. They have a hymn—"

"Yes. We are in the process of having one composed—"

"Well don't. Use the National anthem, *Amhrán na bhFiann*.

That'll strike a chord in almost all of the crowd with its nostalgia and rightness. It will help focus *their* loyalties and *their* sense of self. We're talking about the Kerry team here, a local team and a local focus is the thing right now, a familiarity that will get the nationalistic juices flowing. The *Danann* have not yet built up an identity of belonging to anybody except Curran. They're still characters from Marvel Comics. Still Hollywood fodder. Unworldly. So the national anthem will go for that jugular."

He burst into song and John-Joe was moved in spite of himself.

"*Faoi mhóid bheith saor, Seantír ár sinsear feasta,*" McGarrity went on "Sworn to be free, No more our ancient sire land. Shit. It even brings tears to my eyes. 'Sire land'. That's a good phrase. Are you still with me?"

John-Joe was staring off into the middle distance but his mind was still involved with McGarrity's explanations.

"Yes. Yes, I am," he blurted out. "I was astounded when I first travelled to Dublin. I was what?... about fifteen... and when I played hurling against a Dublin team, I – we – were treated as if we were from a different planet. Our accents, the way we looked – we played so badly."

"That's how it works. Social identities, they're so powerful. And they have an inbuilt exclusivity factor which used to be thought of as innate – something we are born with and psychologists focused on individual characteristics when tackling otherness but now you have to look at social identities; established social categories within societies; cultural, ethnic, gender, class identities and how we want to be seen by others."

"If I'm understanding you, the Dubliners' behaviour stemmed from how they wanted to be seen by me?"

"Yes. Their self-image was based upon your reactions and their self-reflection."

"And if I hadn't reacted... respectfully – which I did – their self-image would have suffered?"

McGarrity looked at John-Joe keenly but said nothing.

"So...," John-Joe carried the thought on "if we don't treat the *Danann* with respect, no, fear, their self-respect will suffer?"

"And their performance. And – here's the trick if you can pull it off – if you can alter the crowd's perception, the *Danann* will diminish. It follows as the night the day."

"So... is this true? Does our, my, the crowd's perception alter theirs?"

"Come on, John-Joe. You've played enough to know that it does. It's a self-reflection, a looking-glass self we're talking about."

John-Joe was striding up and down, excited by the possibilities which McGarrity was revealing to him.

"So we ignore all the hype. Dress like culchies—"

"Badly-fitting shirts, baggy shorts, the old green and gold, terrible haircuts. Lambs to the slaughter."

"We don't react to their flashy entry."

"Ignore them, turn your backs. Show them your arses."

"Lift a leg and fart. Jesus. Vinnie would hate that."

"And be diminished by it."

John-Joe looked ahead.

"How long before we land?"

"Patience, tiger. You'll soon be at them."

24

Outside an old warehouse in Galway, on the banks of the River Corrib, the whooper swans had come down from the North and they cruised, thousands of them, up and down the faintly wind-rippled water. The tide was out and many small boats, some in good condition, many rotting picturesquely, were slumped over on the hard flat mud. The immaculate whiteness of the swans and the lines of their upright necks were out of place against the background of slimy piers, rusting storm drains, dull mud and black water. Along the shore some stooped, two-storey houses were huddled together against the chill of the Atlantic air. Several were painted white, some a dull green and the occasional owner had indulged in a deep rose paint. Clouds, brooding and immense, promised blustery weather.

The warehouse was four shallow stories high, making it the tallest structure in the wide, flat vista. A very tall mast soared from among a clutter of satellite dishes on the roof. The windows were dark and barred and doors were substantial. It was the private domain of a man called Jack.

Jack was one of his many names but with the slight desire

for some sort of normalcy that lurked in the psyches of such as he, all his alias first names started with a J; John, James, Joseph – and all their diminutives. The surnames he used, sparingly over the decades, always started with an M, just as his original, Irish name had. Intelligence agencies all over the world cautioned against such misplaced loyalty among operatives. It made them too easy to trace, the agencies said. Lined up on paper and sorted by the simplest word processing system, the double initials left too clear a path, the agencies exclaimed. In spite of the undisputed logic of what the agencies said and in spite of the pressure brought to bear on the operatives by the agencies, the operatives, by and large, resorted to the practice regularly. Perhaps it was their way of holding onto some sense of self in the midst of all the duplicity and double-dealing.

The same held even more true amongst the assassins. All the *nom de guerre* they adopted and changed with each newly-created identity either started with the same letter or fell into the same category; of animals, or places or classic allusions. Since an operative out there in deep cover was on his or her own and since they were, for the most part, beyond the help of any of the agencies in time of trouble, the agencies advised but did not insist. Whatever helped the operatives cope with the immense psychological pressure was ultimately acceptable.

So Jack it was and had been ever since he had distanced himself from The Company. Not totally, death was the only way to achieve that, but effectively. The Company called on his services at irregular intervals, knowing that Jack was still useful but not as malleable as a full-time operative should be. He had carried out too many orders for them. Risked all he had too many times. Gone too far and stayed too long, especially in Chile. He had done things there that the nineteenth-century Fenian, O'Leary had said you must not do for your country. Jack was kept on a looooong, unobtrusive leash.

Jack (he was called Joey then) had also commandeered

The Company's state-of-the-art electronic equipment which he had shipped out of Chile just before it all blew up in their faces. He had secreted it away to a small farm in South Africa and used it as the basis of a one-man industry. The Company allowed this, knowing that it would prove useful in the future. He had refined it and updated it and kept it at the front edge of surveillance and data-manipulation technology. This was easily done under the pall of the apartheid government of the time. If you were part of the substrata of deception and respected on the operational as against the political level, then it was sublimely easy to access, or even develop the latest technology. Joey (he was known as Jimmy there) gained, had earned, such respect and, consequently, all the doors to all the laboratories and factories in the shadowy underworld of apartheid South Africa opened to him. Once you were on the inside, he found out, the highly secret stuff of subterfuge was tossed about with astounding abandon. Microchip capacity? You need that factory on the Witwatersrand. Microwave testing facilities? Just go see Piet at this address. Digital image enhancement? Isn't old Frikkie doing that? Here's his personal number. And the new crowd? The same as the old crowd – different skin for the most part. And just as secretive. The political world – all the world over – just loved secrecy. Thrived on it. It came with the territory, a plump security blanket behind which… well, we'll never really know will we? That's its purpose. No matter how each regime came to power on the promise of open, transparent government, the securocrats remained, buried deeper, disowned by all but the firmly entrenched, impervious to the pressure groups, convinced that any party which came to power would need them, more and more as the world turned and the technology developed.

After many decades, the cornucopia of covert technology and material development had ceased to amaze Jack. He swore by Negroponte's prediction that each branch of technology in the fourth revolution would double in power and halve in price every few years. One weekend, at a braai, he happened to mention to his host, the production manager of an electronics manufacturer in Cape Town, that he would love to investigate a specific ceramic for its sound carrying attributes. He had read a paper on the subject in a journal issued by the Massachusetts Institute of Technology and yearned to know more about it. His host, a bluff Afrikaner with the most revolting haircut on a human head, had pounded him on the back and boomed "No problem! Just get ready to fly out of here on Monday."

So out of Cape Town he flew on Monday, into a fairyland of technology. The laboratory was buried in a mountain. The bonhomie and easy chat of his guide - a sales representative from the electronics firm - with the armed guards at the entrance gate was relaxed and friendly. It was all in Afrikaans and there were several ribald stories or anecdotes exchanged, which his guide did not attempt to translate. All Jimmy had to do to gain admission, was to give the number of one of his US passports, pose for a photograph and sign an incomprehensible document. Down inside the mountain, it was very serious. Vast amounts of apartheid money had been thrown at the research and development of a veritable cocktail of substances. Whole research labs or development plants had been either imported or replicated from all over the world. He even found out that there was a nuclear accelerator on the next level and that the results of tests there were regularly sent to companies all over the developed world. The person in charge of ceramic research was fresh out of the University of Cape Town, with a degree in science *cum laude*. He was pimply, intense and on first-name terms with scientists and technicians in some of the world's foremost institutions and companies. Jimmy soon found out that key aspects of the MIT paper had been based on research done by this youth but the youth seemed unaffected by this. This was his first job and, having no other work experience to compare it with, assumed that this international reciprocity was the norm. It was only when Jimmy rashly mentioned the world's reluctance to deal with South Africa that the youth bristled and a strange brand of schizophrenic patriotism brought his pimples to a state of eruption.

Having built one of the foremost monitoring stations outside of the US, Jimmy was poised to take full advantage of satellite transmission as was used regularly by the South African government and the emerging African National Congress. He was able to keep abreast of sensitive and secret political developments. Indeed, he was often the conduit for reports on the relevant meetings. This allowed him to relocate his facility before the change of political regime threatened to make him an embarrassment. He moved lock, stock and barrel to Galway and remained there, working for whomever could afford him and remaining totally and utterly objective. Quirk had used him regularly over the years. So had the organisations and government departments against which Quirk was wont to strive. Now Jack (as he was known in Ireland) was considered the most reliable facility in Western Europe.

25

Kitty got out of the limo and it pulled smoothly away from the warehouse. She approached the door pressed a button on the keypad, glancing up at the camera lens tucked into the corner of the door jamb.

"Yes? Can I help you?" asked a thin, metallic voice.

"I'm Kitty Ring. Mr Quirk sent me."

"Come in."

The door opened and standing immediately inside was a sandy-haired man in a rumpled tracksuit. He had that deep golden tan that Irish skin never seems to be able to acquire and brilliant blue eyes that surveyed her carefully. His handclasp was firm as he shook her hand and pulled her gently through the doorway, his eyes flickering up and down the quayside.

"Follow me, please," he said as he walked across the rather dark interior to a gleaming door at the back. As he punched a code into the keypad, Kitty saw that the door was steel and it slid back into the wall with a quiet hiss of compressed air. They stepped inside and the door closed behind them. The silence was so intense that she felt as if her ears had popped. The man ascended a flight of rubber-coated stairs.

"Quirk said it was very important," he said over his shoulder.

"It is and I need to view it as soon as possible, Mr…?"

"Jack will do. I'm sure we can arrange a viewing."

They were at another steel door, with another keypad. The stairs up which they had come had a slight dogleg in it, so the lower door was out of sight below them. Jack punched another code in and that door opened to reveal a tiny anteroom painted white all over the walls, ceiling and floor. They stepped inside and the door hissed closed behind them. Jack moved towards a row of shelves above a bench and took down a folded white garment.

"This should fit," he said, handing it to her. "There are hats and overshoes there."

Kitty donned the white coat, slipping the card out of her pocket into the pocket of the coat before buttoning it up. She followed Jack's example as he took a paper hat and pulled it on so that all his hair was covered. She had to tuck her hair up under the hat and he watched her as she did so. Then they both slipped on paper shoes over their footwear and Jack opened the inner door. A surge of air reached them and she caught her breath.

"We keep the air pressure high in here. It helps keep the dust out," he said and walked in through the door.

Kitty looked around and thought of the wistful longing of the TV repairman in Tralee. Dominating the large room was the beige bulk of an enormous mainframe computer – or computers – she had no idea which. A faint, deep hum came from this behemoth and the side facing the door was twinkling with hundreds of lights of different colours. On benches around the rooms were dozens of video and audio monitors. Some had white-clad operators seated in front of them. Others were being checked by men or women walking up and down in front of them. One wall was covered in video screens which displayed images varying from flashing columns of figures, through oscillating lines, columns and waves, up to full-colour images of wide, incomprehensible places and people. Each person – and there must have been at least twenty of them – was wearing a combined ear and microphone contraption into which they were quietly talking. The air of concentration was intense and no more than one or two glances came their way as they walked in.

Jack led the way to the back of the room to a cubicle with shoulder-high walls. Inside was a complicated edit suite, fed by a tall bank of players next to the desk. Jack sat on one of the swivel chairs and held out his hand. Kitty took the card from her pocket and gave it to him. With a quick glance, he inserted it into one of the players and started to push buttons and tweak level controls.

"Do you want to make a protection copy?" he asked without looking at her. "We can keep it here while you do what you have to with this one."

"Will it be safe here?" she asked.

He turned and looked at her and she regretted the question.

"A copy would be a good idea, providing—" she said.

"The copy will be catalogued and kept in the vault and nobody will eyeball it without express permission from you or Mr Quirk. We have a lot of sensitive material here. We know how to safeguard it."

She nodded dumbly as he took another card out of a drawer and inserted it into a second player.

"OK," he said. "There's the play button. This wheel will allow you to move backwards and forwards on the recording. There's the pause button and, when you're ready to copy, just select this high-speed option and press the copy button. Do I need to repeat that?"

"No. I work with computers. Nothing as impressive as this of course."

"Of course. I'll leave you to it. Just pick up this phone and ask for me when you're finished. I'll take you through the exit procedure."

He stood and offered her earphones. She took them and sat down. Wiping her hands on the white coat she pressed the reverse button. There was a faint click and the LED read 'Start.' Jack left the cubicle as she pressed the play button and leaned forward.

26

McGarrity handed John-Joe a small fishing rod, with a spinner attached as the barge pulled clear of Killaloe Harbour and then he sat on the gunwale, his foot resting on the long, iron tiller. John-Joe sat opposite him enjoying the cool breeze that came downstream and watching his fishing line create a thin white wake in the black, rippled water. They both had a can of beer within easy reach. They soon left the slight bustle of Killaloe behind and entered a wide stretch of placid water framed by purple and green weeds, from which came the twittering of river birds as the weeds nodded in the wake of the barge. A sizzling line of sapphire blue sprang into existence and then vanished again just as suddenly as it moved upstream against the reeds. A kingfisher was about its business. Further along, on a tiny strip of river mud, poised on one leg, the other curled up against its breast a heron stood staring intently into the water at its next meal. McGarrity broke the companionable silence

"In marketing, positioning is everything. Your team has been positioned, through no fault of your own, as the underdogs, in this match. It's a good position and it generates a lot of sympathy. The trick is to turn sympathy, which is a passive emotion, into something more positive, anger, or, better still, rage. Rage is good. I can do a lot with rage."

"This is a sport, remember," said John-Joe, feeling uncomfortable.

"Sport? There was very little sport on the field for the inaugural game."

"Oh. You saw that then?"

"Saw it? I studied it."

"Why?"

"Because of that shit, Switzer. Jesus I hate him. He's good though."

"Who's he?"

"Curran's secret weapon. A marketing genius. He keeps a crumpled bullet on his desk."

"What on earth for?"

"A bullet represents deadliness, a crumpled bullet represents impregnability."

"But how did it get crumpled?"

"Nobody knows but it doesn't matter. The imagery is enough. Switzer does his best work just below the rational level. He's good above it, what with great events, great promotions and great advertising. But below, in the shadow at the edge of emotions, he's… he's almost as good as me. You've got a bite."

The rod had indeed bent and the line in the water was moving across the current. John-Joe activated the reel gear and started to ease the line in.

"It's pretty powerful," he said.

"Probably a pike. Let the rod do the work."

John-Joe raised the rod upright and the whipping motion increased. McGarrity reached for the line and tugged gently at it.

"Medium size. Haul away."

John-Joe did as he was told and a respectable looking pike started to break the surface. When it came up to the boat,

McGarrity reached down and grasped the fish behind its head, in front of the dorsal fin. He unhooked the fish and held it up to the light.

"Don't know why we bother. We can't eat them and they don't really put up a good fight." He held the fish up to his mouth and said, in a stage whisper. "Not like John-Joe Crosby in his first new-style hurling match." He released the fish back into the water and turned to face John-Joe.

"I watched you closely," said McGarrity. "Because you were on the cusp between sportsmanship and all-out war. You very nearly lost it, especially towards the end but something stopped you turning into an out-and-out animal. What was it, do you think?"

"I suppose," said John-Joe slowly. "That it was a lifetime of training with the emphasis on tough but fair play."

"Whatever it was, it made me realise that the game could be turned up a notch or two in the violence stakes without losing its soul. That's its difference from Curran's mayhem. That's what will get the crowds on your side. That's why I volunteered to help you in your marketing."

"And how would you do that?"

"Word of mouth to start with."

John-Joe looked sceptical.

"It's no use looking down your nose," said McGarrity. "Word of mouth, properly managed can confirm a devotee in his or her faith and can engineer an attitude shift in any community, even the one that Curran has created out of fuckall with one match and a lot of fulfilled expectations. It will help us defuse the powerful attraction of the lumpen proletariat that he has tapped into and harnessed so effectively. That's what we did up North. That's how we stopped the violence. Seriously. We laid the groundwork for the ceasefire and the subsequent disarmament by making violence a very uncool activity, in all age groups. We spread rumours, reports, jokes, feel-good stories, all slanted subtly against the hard men. We had a workshop in Tuscany with a team of the best Irish and English comedy writers. The funniest men and women we could find. I even had a song written that should have won a Grammy."

"A song!"

"Aye. A song, written by a well-known singer, who shall be nameless, because his fans would never forgive him. It was called *The Orange Hoor and the Fenian Git.*"

"I've heard that."

"Of course you have. It was so indescribably filthy that it sped around Ireland like lightning."

John-Joe started to sing

"They came across a plump young girl
In a field in Enniskillen
Said the Orange Hoor, 'You know I'm sure
We could have her for a shillin."
How does it go? They both sang;

"Soooooooo *they shed their load in the middle of the road*
And they went away contented."

"That's it. That's the clean part," said McGarrity, roaring with laughter. "It worked wonders. 'Orange Hoor' and 'Fenian Git' became almost terms of endearment after a while. I was very proud of that. I deflated prejudice in an unbelievable way. Football teams were formed with the names and they played against each other. Soon the extremists were satirised so much that they became totally unmotivated. It's hard to be full of rant and hatred when everybody is laughing at you. People had forgotten the integral humour of the Irish and the Scottish planters too. There was a toast my Grandaddy used to trot out every Christmas."

McGarrity stood up and addressed the waters, the reeds and the odd passing boat; "Here's to the great and immortal William of Orange. Who saved us from rogues and roguery, knaves and knavery, popes and popery, brass buckles and wooden shoes. And may anyone who denies this toast be rammed, crammed and jammed into the great gun of Athlone, and the gun fired into the pope's belly, and the pope into the devil's belly and the devil into hell, and the door locked and the key in a Protestant's pocket. And may we never lack a brisk Protestant boy to kick the arse of a papist. And here's a fart for the Bishop of Cork."

McGarrity toasted the surrounding land and riverscape and sucked on his beer.

"That humour is still there. It was buried a while through fear of the 'other' but now it's back. And this is just a few years since a Southern Ireland Cabinet Minister was castigated and nearly excommunicated, for singing the *Ould Orange Flute* at a public dinner. Here's to humour. Long may it make us all laugh."

"So how would you apply all that to us?"

"For a start we would take all the *Danann* players, with their ferocious nicknames and devise humorous versions of them. Change 'ferocious' to 'flatulent', 'awesome' to 'arsehole', that sort of thing. Start rumours about them abusing children, their mothers, their sisters. Accuse them of being transvestites, cross-dressers, cuckolds, arsonists. We'll even manufacture a touch of corruption – throwing a match for money. That sort of thing."

"Will anybody believe it?"

"A few will to begin with. More will when Curran and his players start strenuously denying the accusations. Once the target of an outrageous lie starts to deny it, the people start to believe the lie in direct proportion to the sincerity of the denial. The intention is to damage the image of invincible superheroes. Make them look very human, venal and a bit ridiculous. There are rumours about the corruption involved in Arena21. We'll resuscitate them and see how far we can get with that."

"It all sounds expensive," said John-Joe.

"Sure it's expensive but I can do it on a lot less than Switzer has to play with. And Quirk is willing to pay."

"That TV commercial? The one at the game? Did Switzer create that?"

"No. But he approved it. And what a turkey!" McGarrity laughed again.

"It didn't work?"

"No. How could it, with a name like The Great American Shoe Company?"

"What do you mean?"

"I mean that if you ask the buyers of expensive sports shoes anywhere in the world, especially in the States, who the Great American Shoe Company is, who do you think they'll name?"

"I don't know. Nike?"

"There's Nike, there's Converse, there's Adidas, they all exude an American identity, they could all claim the title – and they're all made in fucking China. Nike was foremost in the consumers' minds so, while The Great American Shoe Company's products were blocking the warehouses, glutting the outlets – and bankrupting them too, because retailers all over the world paid huge premiums for stocking the shoes – Nike shoes were walking out of the stores by themselves. That's what happened. The research proved it after the event and it could have prevented it beforehand. The positioning was great but the branding was terrible. A simple recall test in that fucking insane state of theirs, Califuckingfornia, could have sorted it out. The sales of Nike are going through the roof and the Great American Shoe Company is going under. Hell. I love marketing. It's obscenely enjoyable."

McGarrity's baritone boomed out over the water as the shoreline fell away on each side and the white-dappled waves of Loch Derg opened up before their eyes.

"So they flashed their stones to a bugger in Clones
And they both earned sixpence farthing."

27

The picture that appeared on the main screen was in black and white and the contrast was very high. A quick search of the desk and Kitty found the contrast controls. She fiddled with them until the picture was in clear crisp colour. A succession of white letters and numerals whizzed along a black strip at the top of the screen and a date and time code appeared across the bottom of the screen. The recording had been made three weeks before Tomas died.

It was a bird's eye view of an empty office and nothing was happening. She went into fast forward and the time code whirred around for several minutes then a figure entered the office and crossed it at high speed. She stopped and rewound back to the point of the figure's entry. It was Curran.

"Christ, Tomas," she breathed. "How the hell did you set this up?"

Curran crossed to a cupboard which she could see had a one-way mirror door. He opened it and fiddled with a piece of equipment inside and closed the door. She reversed the tape and played it again, frame by frame until she caught a glimpse of the equipment inside the cupboard. Then she stopped the tape and studied the icons that ran across the top of the screen. They were sufficiently similar to the icons on her Apple Mac for her to find her way around. She chose the digitising option and punched in code prior to and after the section she wanted to examine. A window opened, with space for a filename. She typed in 'cupboard' and hit 'enter. A clock icon appeared and the hand rotated for several seconds. When it disappeared, she found the file name and played the digitised clip. Again she stopped it at the required frame and grabbed the magnifying glass icon with the mouse. She moved it to centre frame and clicked once. The image got bigger. She clicked again and again until she could see the equipment in the cupboard clearly. It was a camera, pointing out into the office through the mirror door. She returned to the source tape and played it at normal speed. Curran positioned one of the two chairs in front of the desk so that is almost faced the camera directly. He then dragged the other chair to the back wall before taking a seat behind the desk. Moments later the door opened again and a man she recognised as Dougherty came in followed by a man she had seen before but couldn't place. The latter carried a small black bag and he rushed forward to gesture Dougherty into the single chair before moving to stand beside the desk, also facing the camera. He placed the bag on the desk and Dougherty turned his head to look at it. Curran leaned forward and spoke very clearly and evenly.

"What can you do at the next council meeting?" he asked.

"Anything you want," replied Dogherty. "I can even arrange to have several councillors off sick, providing—"

O'Shea, for it was he, pushed the bag forwards and Dogherty grabbed it and squeezed it between his fingers.

"As we agreed?" he asked.

O'Shea nodded but Curran spoke.

"Yes. The sum you stipulated. Now, let's get things clear, shall we? So there's no misunderstanding as to what you have undertaken."

Dougherty nodded.

"You undertake," said Curran carefully. "To arrange it so that the majority of the council will vote for my proposal."

"Don't worry," said Dougherty, kneading the bag. "There's enough here to go around."

"Yes," said Curran. "There certainly is. And you undertake to use the money in that bag to ensure that the really... inconvenient... conditions attached to the tender are dropped." Curran waited until Dougherty replied.

"Yes. OK. Sure," he said.

"And you will ensure that any attempt to raise the material contraventions of the county plan, which my proposal might or might not contain, are ruled out of order."

"When you've chaired as many council meetings as I have—"

"Good," interrupted Curran. "We understand each other. O'Shea, show Mr Dougherty out."

Kitty stopped the tape, rewound it and started a copy of it. Then she dialled Quirk's number and told him what Tomas had recorded.

"Well, well, well," Quirk said when she had finished. "That should be enough to put them away for a while. Now there is only one man you must show that to. He's in Dublin, I'm afraid. Go back to your hotel and find the driver. I'll speak to him in the meantime."

Kitty waited quietly until the full card had been copied. It didn't take long. Then she pocketed both cards and stood up to look around. One of the men saw her and came over.

"Can I help you?" he asked.

"I need to speak to Jack."

He nodded and led the way out of the room. They both divested themselves of the protective clothing and threw it into a bin in the anteroom. They left the room and went downstairs and into the ground floor. Once out through the steel door, he led her across the dim room to a lift door at the side. He opened the door and, stepping politely aside he ushered Kitty in. Then he pressed a button and stepped out as the lift door started to close.

"Jack is always on the roof 'round about now," he said and closed the outer door.

The lift rose smoothly a considerable distance before stopping. She opened the door and stepped out. There was a closed door on one side of the small landing and an open door on the other. Through it she could see the sky. She walked out onto the roof of the warehouse. Jack was seated on a canvas chair next to a small folding table. He was looking intently through a powerful pair of binoculars. At his elbow was an open laptop computer. He turned at the crunching sound of her feet.

"Ah, Miss Ring. Forgive me. I'll only be a moment."

She nodded and walked over to the parapet. Down below, the sweep of the Corrib was dotted with swans. Jack typed fast and smoothly.

"Whooper swans. Migrants from Russia," he said, without looking up. "I helped tag some of them last year and several were tagged at Novya Zemla only months ago. On the legs, so you can only identify the colour of the tags when they are on shore. It's nice to see them back again. Good numbers this year. I've a soft spot for migrants, having been one myself for a long time."

He stood, walked over to her and offered her the binoculars. She took them and focused on the swans. They were very powerful glasses and a glistening bird filled her vision. It was beautiful as it moved slowly and regally through the dark water.

"They used to be called Bewick's swan," Jack said. "After the famous illustrator. Recently they found that they were different species, in fact the same species as the Tundra or whistling swan. They're not, perhaps as graceful as the mute swan. The curves of their necks leaves a little to be desired."

"Are they really mute?"

"No, they're not, in spite of the name. Nor is there such a thing as a 'swan song.'"

"Pity."

"A great pity. Legend and poetry demand that there should be.

He suddenly began to recite in an attractive baritone voice;

"The silver swan, who living had no note
When death approached unlocked her silent throat
Rested her breast against the reedy shore
Thus sang her first and last and sang no more
Farewell all joy. Come death and close mine eyes
More geese than swans now live
More fools than wise."

"That's lovely," said Kitty. "Who wrote it?"

"Our old friend anonymous. Was the recording interesting?"

"Dynamite."

"Incriminating?"

"Very."

"Then I don't think you should carry it anywhere."

"I've got to show it to… some people."

"I know and I have a way to make it accessible to you, at any time. These people are all in some official capacity or other?"

"Yes."

"Then they will have access to a computer and the web."

"Of course."

"Then I suggest that we post it on one of my sites. You memorise the URL and a password and you can download it and show it to whom you please. No need for you to carry anything, anywhere. I'll keep the two recordings here so that they can be verified as and when necessary. Acceptable?"

"Yes. Very." Her relief was manifest.

"Excellent. Now, before you continue your journey, which

will most probably be to Dublin, may I treat you to one of the local culinary specialties?"

There was something reassuring about Jack, perhaps it was the expensive tan, maybe it was the calmness that he generated, then again, it may have been the blue eyes.

"And what is that?" she asked.

"Stuffed swan."

She gasped and then laughed. He was joking. He must be joking.

"You're joking!"

"Of course I'm joking. I mean oysters and Guinness. In Spiddal just out of town."

Her stomach rumbled on cue.

The Oysters were splendid and the Guinness smoothed them down superbly and the new moon was lounging on its back, reflected in the still waters of Galway Bay. Replete, they both sipped their coffee and their smoky single malts and gazed alternatively out of the southerly-facing window or at the glowing fire in the huge stone fireplace. She felt very far away from the recent tumult and confusion in her life and then this vivid realisation stirred her conscience as the thought of John-Joe and his troubles stumbled into her mind. Jack noticed her sudden loss of contentment.

"You're troubled."

"Yes. I feel guilty."

"Don't. You needed a respite. You have been in some deeply-troubled water and, I fear, you are heading for more such."

"I know that."

"But you don't know it all, I'm afraid."

She looked at him but was silent.

"You have some idea of Quirk's background?" He saw her stiffen and leaned over the table to touch her hand lightly. "Don't worry. I am not going to say anything against him. I am merely warning you about what you will face when you get to Dublin.

Quirk was heavily involved in the troubles up North and has made some enemies whose ill-will has not dissipated with the current peace. There are men there who dedicated most of their lives to seeking and killing people like Quirk and who are disoriented by the current situation. They are unsure of their ultimate loyalty and, since they have operated outside the law for decades, they remain dangerous. Always were. Always will be. They are thin-skinned recidivists and ready to slip back into the murk of hate and extreme nationalism. You will become involved with such people, so you must be careful."

She sat in silence while he looked anxiously into her eyes.

"OK?" he said.

She finished her whiskey.

"OK."

28

The Kerry team was boarding the Dublin train at Tralee station, under John-Joe's and Joe's anxious eyes. Joe had a list in his hand, ticking off names as the men boarded. Two of the tough men stood next to the carriage door and John-Joe gestured for them to board. They both shook their heads.

"What's on your minds?" asked John-Joe.

"You," said one of the men.

"They're your minders," said Joe.

"Quirk's idea?" asked John-Joe.

One of the men nodded.

"No use farting against thunder," said Joe, boarding the train.

John-Joe grinned wryly and made to board. One of the tough men moved swiftly in front of him and the other almost trod on his heels as he climbed up. They moved in procession along the corridor up to their assigned compartment at the front of the train. Joe entered and took a seat next to the window, as did John-Joe. One of the men sat down directly inside the door and the other closed the door and stood outside it, looking up and down the corridor. The sound of slamming doors was heard and the train lurched slightly.

On the platform, a guard was walking leisurely towards the rear of the train, slamming each open door. As he approached the last carriage, a man came hurrying as fast as he could through the barrier, waving for the train to wait. What was impeding his progress was the fact that he was swinging along on a crutch and most of his right leg was encased in plaster of Paris. This was much scuffed and dirtied around the foot as if he had been wearing it for a long while. The guard stood by the last door, holding it open and waiting for the man to come panting up. He helped him aboard and slammed the door, blowing his whistle the meantime. The train lurched again and slid smoothly out of the station.

Aboard the train, the man with the crutch moved along the corridor towards the front, walking briskly, in spite of his plaster-encased leg. Indeed, it was plain from his movements, that the leg was not injured in the least, the plaster constituting a camouflage designed to elicit casual sympathy and deflect attention. He moved through two carriages before he met anybody and when he did, he immediately slumped onto his crutch and swung awkwardly as before. So he made his way to the last but one carriage from the front before entering a compartment occupied by a middle-aged couple who spared him a cursory glance before returning to their reading matter. The man nodded at them and settled down to patiently bide his time.

The train moved through the Irish countryside and the people on board relaxed into that strange lethargy that is often induced by train travel. In the compartments occupied by the players, the initial buzz of conversation died away except for an occasional comment, mostly ribald. There was a dull sense of repressed tension amongst the hurlers in the team. The tough men, who were all in one compartment, were silent and still. At regular intervals, two of the men would move to the front carriage and relieve the couple guarding John-Joe.

So the afternoon passed and the evening approached. The lights on the train were switched on and, after a slight swirl of movement and rearranging of limbs, most of the players settled back down for the last stretch across the midlands to the capital city. Some of the more restless men headed towards the dining carriage which had a refreshment counter, selling crisps and soft drinks. It was through this small, listless crowd, that the man on the crutch made his apologetic way until he came to the linking causeway to the first carriage. He stood there, motionless, in the shadow next to the toilet, watching the man on guard outside John-Joe's compartment. The man was leaning against the window, peering out at the passing lights of villages and the irregular sweep of car headlights across the sky. Suddenly the compartment door opened and John-Joe stepped out. He moved to peer through the window beside the guard.

"Anything worth looking at out there?"

"No," answered the man.

"Go and get some sleep. Everything's fine here."

The man made no answer and John-Joe shook his head and made for the toilet. Short as this exchange was, it was sufficient for the man with the plaster cast to duck into the toilet and disable, with a screwdriver, the door catch which operated the toilet light. He closed over the door and positioned himself astride the toilet seat, one leg on either side. John-Joe stepped inside and two strong hands settled around his neck in a lethal choke hold. The man pushed the door closed with John-Joe's body and increased the pressure of John-Joe's carotid artery and the jugular. As his consciousness slipped away with frightening speed, John-Joe summoned enough strength to kick out at the door. The blow was soft but it was enough to bring the guard to full alert. The next flurry of activities all happened within the space of a few seconds. The guard whistled shrilly. His companion in the compartment hurled himself out into the corridor and Joe followed him out. The man in the toilet slammed the door shut and continued to kill John-Joe, who started to slump to the ground. The guard clasped both hands together, poised on the balls of his feet and sent his hands crashing through the plywood of the door. The strangler, his job nearly done, looked at the gaping hole in amazement. The two hands withdrew and one hand came back immediately, grabbed the strangler's lapels and pulled his face into the door with terrific force. Stunned, he started to slump over John-Joe. The door crashed open and the guardian reached in and whisked the strangler out into the corridor. His companion threw the train door open and slammed his fist into the throat of the stunned strangler who was held in an upright position by his companion. It was a brutal mortal blow that killed the man immediately. The man holding his corpse threw it out of the speeding train and turned to John-Joe who was gasping on the toilet floor. His companion closed the door and went to help.

The intervention had been just in time. John-Joe recovered consciousness and started to raise himself. The man held him down and massaged his throat gently. Joe now reached the toilet.

"What happened?" he gasped.

"Tried to kill him."

"Is he all right?"

"Yes."

John-Joe was all right. He got to his feet with some assistance and put both hands to his neck.

"Where is he?" he asked faintly.

"They threw him out of the train," said a dazed Joe.

"He was trying to kill me. Nearly did, too."

"Jesus. What have we got ourselves into?"

"Trouble," said John-Joe as the train sped on towards Dublin.

29

It was raining heavily when the train pulled into Heuston Station in Dublin. The small crowd which had gathered to welcome the Kerry team had been driven away by the cold and wet. Curran was there, sheltering under a large umbrella, held aloft by an irate and damp O'Shea. Most of the *Danann* team was there, grumbling amongst themselves. The press reporters had retired to the Galway Hooker, the bar in the station precinct, where they waited for a pre-arranged warning call from O'Shea. Three camera teams, with their bulky equipment, were huddled at the back of the train shed with their cameras swathed in plastic sleeves. They were chain-smoking and the cameraman from RTE was holding forth.

"Bleeding wanker. Thinks he's James Fucking Cameron. We were up in a cherry picker, swaying in the wind. The rain was worse than this and he's trying to coax a bleeding pigeon into the frame. The pigeon's huddled into a dry corner and is not about to come out into that downpour. He tries bread, tries sugar but the pigeon is saying 'no bleeding way'. The stunt man, what's his name from Scotland? You know, the mad cunt. Yeah, that's right, MacDonald, he's standing there in pyjamas, ready to

LEABHARLANN
CO. CILL DARA

leap out and he's bleeding furious because the cardboard boxes he's going to land on are softening in the rain and the pigeon's comafuckingtose and the bread and sugar are dissolving and I'm thinking there must be an easier way to earn a living."

The others nodded, absorbing that tale into the collective memory of cameramen everywhere. The wry (invariably male) practitioners of image capture, they looked down on presenters as merely unskilled talking heads, sound engineers as necessary evils on a shoot – especially ENG (Electronic News Gathering) shoots. As for directors, they were beneath contempt, no-talent, self-indulgent and self-deluding wankers, the lot of them. One of them flipped his cigarette end onto the track and spat after it.

"Anybody got work at Arena21?"

Another answered.

"Nah! They don't fucking want cameramen there. They just want operators to sit at a desk and fiddle with the controls."

"What controls?" asked the youngest.

"The switches that operate the cameras."

"But the union says—"

"The union can say what it wants, that bleeder Curran isn't listening."

"But all the matches are going to be broadcast and that means cameras."

The rest was a desultory litany from each of them in turn.

"Yeah. But these cameras are all automatic."

"High speed cameras up and down the sidelines."

"And four on wires across the stadium."

"Ten above the stands. On drones."

"*Sixteen* above the stands on drones."

"OK! Sixbleedingteen!"

"All self-focusing."

"All operated by wankers in the edit suite."

"Criminal."

"Wojus."

"What do you reckon on these bleeding columns, then?" asked one who was standing in the slender shelter of a slim iron column.

"Italian, I should say."

"Terazzo, I think it's called."

"Palazzo, for crysake!"

You're mistaking me for someone who gives a fuck. Terazzo, palazzo, pizza. That Italian shit is all the same."

"Doesn't suit the Irish climate anyway."

"Irish climate! There's no discernible climate in this fucking country."

"Pulled a gig in Cape Town last year. Now *that's* a climate."

"Here's the train."

"Thanks be to the suppuratin' Christ."

The train pulled slowly into the station, in among the columns, the balustrades, decorative urns and flower garlands, all glistening in the rain. The camera crews moved up among the waiting *Danann* players and readied their gear. O'Shea made a quick call on his mobile phone. With a dull shriek, the train stopped and the doors clattered open. Joe was the first to alight, followed by John-Joe, who was still bracketed by two of the tough men. Curran moved forwards and Joe went to meet him. Curran spoke first.

"Well, do you think your team is up to scratch?"

"Scratch is it?" said Joe. "They'll scratch all right. Scratch the hides off some of your men."

Curran turned towards the RTE cameraman, who was closest to him, the light from the sungun casting deep shadows on his face.

"An estimated fifty million people will be watching this match all over the world," he said. "The *Danann* website is in danger of crashing, thanks to the traffic and the betting. Whatever the outcome of this match, the great game will be changed utterly and beyond all recognition."

He stopped and held his face still and expressionless, knowing the value of a good sound and vision byte. The camera turned to Joe who, in spite of his efforts to look impassive, wrinkled his eyes against the glare. The other reporters were gathering around the focal point of the meeting.

"We're ready to give of our best. I have never seen the like of this team. Kerry – what am I saying – all Ireland will be proud of these boys next Saturday."

The reporters, with tape recorders and notebooks crowded around them and began a barrage of questions. The Kerry team was almost all on the platform and squaring up to the *Dananns*. There was much scowling and nudging between the two teams and the trainers moved up and down, keeping them apart. The two tough men had kept John-Joe towards the back, away from any potential flash point.

Suddenly a dark figure slipped noiselessly from behind a column and darted towards John-Joe. A knife blade flashed in the light but he wasn't nearly quick enough. One of the men grasped his wrist and twisted it in a wide circle which forced the upper arm up and out of the shoulder socket. The other tough man moved to the far side of the would-be assassin and, reaching out grabbed the arm of his colleague. They both crouched and slammed their bodies towards each other, with the man, now on his tiptoes in between. John-Joe turned towards them at the sound of crunching bones and imploding lungs. He saw the two tough men straighten, with the man slumped between them like a rag doll whose feet rose as they left the ground. The two of them moved into the shadows towards a large rubbish bin. Swiftly, they raised the lid and threw the limp body in headfirst. Then they both turned and gently ushered John-Joe back in amongst the Kerry team.

30

It was night-time when the limo reached Dublin. It had rained as they were driving all across Ireland and Kitty discovered that the driver was even more taciturn than any of Quirk's other men. Since one mile of damp, restless hedgerow looks very much like another and the Guinness and whiskey she had imbibed was still in her system, she dozed off before they reached the Shannon and came to only when the car stopped and the driver grunted and opened the door.

A chill blast of air and a fine mist of rain destroyed the cosiness of the luxurious interior and she shook herself and stepped out into the night. They had stopped directly outside a discreet door in one of the enormous government buildings that brood in the purlieus of Dawson Street. The driver walked to the door and stood patiently in front of it. Kitty stood beside him.

A voice issued from a speaker in the dark doorway.

"These premises are closed. Please call back during office hours."

The driver raised his head so that the light from the nearby street lamp illuminated his features. He turned it from side to side, displaying each profile. There was a crisp, metallic click and the door opened. The driver stepped through and Kitty followed him. The door closed behind them and the click was louder and even more metallic. So was the voice; "Your business?"

"To see Setanta," replied the driver.

"There's nobody here with that name."

The driver waited impassively. The metallic voice gave in first.

"Who are you?"

"Your computer files will tell you that any second now. This is Kitty Ring and she has something to show Setanta."

"Only Setanta," said Kitty bravely but she didn't feel very brave.

They stood waiting. The driver's calmness reassured Kitty but what happened next made her jump. A door burst open and three large men ran in through it. Two of them brutally grabbed the driver who made no resistance, although he looked as if he could have.

"You murdering bastard," said one of the men. "Got you at last."

They dragged him back through the door as the third man grabbed Kitty's arm in a vice-like grip.

"Hey! Let go. I want to see Setanta," she yelled as the man dragged her after the others. "Do you hear?"

There was no reply. Indeed, nobody spoke as Kitty and the driver were dragged along a dark passage and up a wide flight of marble stairs. The only sound was of heavy breathing and the click of her heel on the steps. All the men, she realised, had rubber-soled shoes. The silence made their roughness all the more threatening. At the top of the stairs, the driver was dragged off to one side while she was dragged straight on towards the back of the building. She was dragged past the imposing double doors, down the corridor to where the doors were more modest and business-like, with plates on them. They stopped outside one marked 'Research' and she was bundled through unceremoniously.

There was a heavy wooden table in the centre of the brightly-lit room, with two chairs on either side. A small bed covered in dark blankets stood in a corner and a large mirror was mounted, dead centre, on one wall. Another man, with a brutal crew cut sat at the table and he glared at Kitty as she was pushed into a chair facing him.

"What do you want here?" he asked. The man who had brought her stood at the side of the table, with his arms folded, a posture that raised his trapezius muscles like bat wings. A real macho pose, 'If he's trying to impress me,' she thought, 'he must feel very inadequate'. In response she tried to look tough.

"I want to see Setanta," she said and it came out steadily if a little too high.

"There is no Mr Setanta here."

"Oh, for Christ sake! I know it's a silly code name. I have something to show him."

Crewcut held out his hand and when she didn't move, snapped his fingers. Still she didn't move. The standing man reached out and put a chokehold on her neck. It wasn't very painful but the room grew dim and she couldn't move. With his other hand he patted her body, straight to the breasts of course. The ease with which he did it was humiliating. It also made her furious.

"You bastards. I don't have it on me and nobody sees it except Setanta."

"Why?" asked Crewcut.

"Because I was told I can trust nobody in this fucking department – whatever the fuck it is – except Setanta."

"Who told you that?"

"Dennis Quirk."

They exchanged glances but said nothing.

"It's safe where you'll never find it. If I fall, someone else will take it to Setanta."

They exchanged glances again and whispers, then the seated one rose and they both left the room. She heard a key turn in the lock. She thought of the URL and password Jack had given her and then looked nervously at the mirror, in case… She didn't know in case of what.

"'If I fall'!" she said. "Jesus! I'm stuck in some third rate movie."

She looked around the room. It had a sterile, very professional look about it. The bright lights were let into the ceiling and protected by sheets of glass. The chair and tables, she saw, were firmly bolted to the floor and the mirror had a dimness to it.

"One-way mirror," she thought. "Shit. Bastards," she said and went to the door. When she hammered on it with her fist, she felt its solidity. She slipped off a shoe and hammered with that. It didn't sound much louder but it made her feel a little better.

"Hey! Hey!" she shouted. "Let me out you bastards."

She looked at the lock. It didn't appear too intimidating. She took clip out of her hair and jammed it in the keyhole. It immediately snapped off.

"Bloody movies," she said and moved to peer at the mirror. Shading her eyes, she could discern shadows and masses but no detail of any sort. She watched for some sign of a moving body but there was none. She ran her fingers around the edge of the glass which stood proud of the wall by about an inch. Tentatively she pulled at it and broke a fingernail.

"Bastards!" she shouted. "Now you're in real trouble."

There was no sound so she went to the bed and threw herself on it. The blanket was hard and horrible and smelled faintly of sweat and vomit and she started to feel really frightened. Up until now it had been unreal and quite exciting and she realised that she had been experiencing it as if it was a movie, with an exciting cast and exciting things happening. Up until now people; Quirk, Jack, even the TV repairman in Tralee had been trying to help her but these men were hard, soulless and impersonal. Who were they? Police of some sort, probably, an anti-IRA squad, gunning for the likes of Quirk who, it was common knowledge, had operated some kind of paramilitary wing in Northern Ireland. There were killers in such ranks and any law enforcement agency which went after them had to resort to brutal tactics. What were they doing to that driver right now? They looked as if they meant to kill him.

And John-Joe? And Tomas? The tears prickled her eyelids and she wiped them away. And Kitty? In spite of herself, she fell asleep.

31

The Kerry team was lodged in an hotel in the same neighbourhood as Arena21. Joe was in John-Joe's room, sipping a black Bushmills. Two men were on guard outside the room.

"Those guys never seem to want sleep," said John-Joe.

"Aye. They're a hard lot. Too hard for the game."

"Hard enough for the *Danann*. That's why Quirk got them for us."

"But what are we doing with the game?"

"Saving it from Curran."

"I'm not so sure. The genie is out of the box. The game will never go back to what it was. You see how the people like it?"

"I've been doing a lot of thinking about this, thanks to Li," said John-Joe, sipping the whiskey. "According to him, we can play the *Danann* on equal terms but not in equal fashion. If we pull it off, we'll save hurling. Make it a game that we can all be proud of and let Curran's style find its own niche, its own audience, which won't be ours." Joe was intrigued but looked sceptical. "You're right," John-Joe carried on "This violent, crowd-pleasing way of playing will never go away. It's the same in all sports. Once a new exciting version of a game, any game, is demonstrated the game changes. Kerry Packer knew that people felt they hadn't got time for five-day test cricket, so he came up with super cricket, limited overs and one-day matches and people loved it. Although five-day matches are still the acme of cricket. Over a hundred years ago, the players of rugby in Northern England wanted compensation for lost wages, so rugby league was born."

"But—" Joe started to say.

"And don't tell me rugby league isn't brutal," John-Joe carried on. "Teddy Roosevelt nearly abolished it by edict when he saw a game back in 1905. So American football was born – body armour and with forward passes that some said would destroy the game. Funnily enough rugby has come back into fashion in the States because college football is too disciplined, too professional."

"What has that got to do with hurling?"

"Everything. What's important is to separate this new style, highly professional – if brutal – away from the school and club playing, where everybody can participate. Look at professional tennis, with its supersonic serves. Who can aspire to them? But it doesn't stop club tennis being strong all over the world."

"But the violence!"

"Yeah, well. I can't say that I don't find it attractive."

"There you are!" said Joe triumphantly "It's not the game, it's the violence. That's the danger."

"What I would hope to achieve," said John-Joe slowly. "Is to become somebody in this style game, a counterbalance to Curran, and eliminate some of the excesses he's brought in. I've been working on that with the team – making space in the game for our style of playing, even in the midst of Curran's style. But the game that will emerge if I succeed will be different to the game you played all your life. It will have evolved, Joe, as all good games should. You better get used to that idea."

Joe looked hard at him but said nothing. His nephew had

never shown such calm authority before. He had watched him grow up but he hadn't noticed this new maturity. This was the first time he'd called him Joe. Not Uncle Joe. He sighed and sipped his drink. Maybe it *was* time to let this new generation build its own game.

"Where's Kitty?" John-Joe suddenly said. "We should have heard from her by now."

"Hopefully she's shown that video to somebody trustworthy."

"In Dublin!" John-Joe snorted.

"Quirk knows the right people."

"Then why isn't he here?"

"He told me a while ago that he never comes to Dublin. It's too dangerous."

"Why, for God's sake?"

"Now that's a question I'd never ask Dennis Quirk," said Joe, finishing his drink. "I'm off to bed. Get some sleep yourself."

"I will. Goodnight."

Joe left and John-Joe sat there quietly. There was a gentle tap on the door.

"Come in," John-Joe called.

The door opened and Tim stood there looking sheepish. John-Joe rose to his feet.

"Tim. Come in and have a drink. I was just thinking about you."

Tim came in and sat on the bed.

"Were you?" he asked. "That'd be unusual, I'd say."

"Tim. Is that a way to talk to an old friend?"

I thought we *were* friends. But lately you've been… distant."

"I've had things to do Tim. You know that. You think it's easy getting a scratch team up to the same level as the *Danann*?"

"Down to the same level might be a—"

"Don't finish that sentence. I thought you were with me in this."

"I am, but…"

"Stay with me, Tim. I need you."

"It doesn't look as if you need anyone in this crusade."

"You're right. It is a crusade. And a price will have to be paid. This game is going to be a rough one. People will get hurt. If you're scared to face the *Danann*, now's the time—"

"I'm not scared! It's just that I don't approve of all the techniques we've been learning."

"It's a bit bloody late for scruples. If you feel you're not up to it, step down, we'll use one of the subs."

"There you go again!" Tim threw his hands in the air. "You've changed."

"Well, of course I've changed. I've had to. I've played Curran's game, I've been chased by thugs, twice somebody tried to kill me and now Kitty—"

"And that's another thing, Kitty."

"What about Kitty?" John-Joe was speaking very quietly and his eyes were narrowed.

"You come to Dublin and within days, you've taken my girl."

"Your girl!" John-Joe was genuinely astounded. "Kitty was nobody's girl when I met her. If you had any claim on her affections, believe me, she didn't know about it. She's straight and she would have told me."

Tim was silent.

"How was she your girl?" John-Joe was insistent.

"Well. I was… getting 'round to asking her."

"Getting 'round to it? For Christ sake, you were living in her house for over a year!"

"Well, what with things and…"

"And what? What?"

"And Tomas."

"What about Tomas?" This was said very softly and John-Joe's eyes were very narrow.

"Well, they were close."

"So…?"

"Unusually close."

Suddenly John-Joe's left forearm was at the back of Tim's neck, his right forearm at his Adam's apple, with all four fingers locked over the left forearm. The pressure on Tim's throat was excruciating and John-Joe's eyes, now mere slits, were in inch from his.

"If you ever say another word against MY girl, I'll snap your neck like a twig."

He released the pressure and dropped his arms. Tim massaged his neck.

"You would, too, wouldn't you?" he said.

"Get out."

Tim left the room and John-Joe threw himself onto the bed, his arm across his eyes. Tim would be OK. He'd let off steam but would fall in line. They all would. He wondered about Kitty. He felt very lonely.

32

It was the same discreet door in the same government building near Dawson Street only this time, Dennis Quirk stood outside, with the light from the street lamp falling across his raised face. He'd stayed away from Dublin - and Setanta - for a long time, knowing that old scars hurt and are susceptible to scratching. He knew Setanta well, had studied him, anticipated him and occasionally out-manoeuvred him, but a chapter in Ireland's destiny was closing, perhaps had closed, and it was time to confront his nemesis and see if he could move on, if not in tandem, then in peace. The door clicked open and he stepped through to face four men, all in combat crouches, all with guns aimed at him.

"Finally," breathed the one with the crew cut.

"Don't get your hopes up, lad. I walked in and I'll walk out. Take me to Setanta."

Crewcut nodded grimly and one of his colleagues, his gun drawn back and up out of reach, approached Quirk and moved around behind him. Quirk obligingly raised his arms as he was quickly and expertly frisked. The frisker stepped back and Quirk stepped forward, heading for the marble staircase. The men nearly fell over themselves, trying to keep him covered. At the bottom of the steps, Quirk stopped and turned. The men barely avoided bumping into each other. It was a deft behavioural supremacy manoeuvre and Quirk had difficulty keeping his face impassive.

"Well?" he snapped.

"Well what?" said Crewcut.

"Which way, lad? Which way? Can't keep Setanta waiting."

Indicating that the others should still keep him covered, Crewcut strode up the stairs and Quirk fell in behind him. In this formation, they wheeled at the top of the stairs and headed for one of the big rooms at the front of the building. Crewcut stopped at a large double door and opened one side of it, half stepping into the room and holding the door halfway open. Quirk stopped and looked at him and the man's eyes dropped. He pushed the door fully opened and stepped back. Quirk entered the room.

The room was splendidly proportion but the furniture was strictly board of works standard issue. Even the chandelier that had once graced the high, embellished ceiling had been replaced by a bare globe in an enamelled shade. Plastic roller blinds covered the two high windows which, judging from the original pelmets which hung there, had once boasted thick velvet curtains. An enormous fireplace with a soaring mantelpiece embraced a photocopying machine and in front of the photocopying machine stood a plain deal table which served as a desk. On the desk was a computer and a telephone. Behind the desk sat a hard-featured man who sized Quirk up and then indicated a chair on the opposite side of the desk. Quirk walked to it and sat down. They looked at each other for a long while.

"I never thought you'd walk in here," said the man in a thick Dublin accent. "You must have friends in high places."

"I have only enemies," replied Quirk. "A much healthier relationship."

"We were *that* close to you."

"It's the last inch that counts."

"Those men of yours, what are they doing now?"

"This and that. I keep them occupied. Africa. Eastern Europe. Nothing for you to worry about. Yours?"

"Drinking mostly?"

"I'm afraid so. It's difficult to keep them up to scratch."

"Yes. Yes, it is."

"You've got one of my men here."

"Yes."

"And a woman."

"Yes."

"What are you doing with them?"

"The woman is… confined for the moment."

"And the man?"

"Well, it seems that some of my men couldn't resist the opportunity to probe a little."

"And settle a few old scores, I daresay."

"I daresay."

"Well, he can handle a little roughing up. I need him back."

"Of course."

"My car is outside."

"He'll be deposited there."

"And the woman?"

"I'll put her in the car with him?"

"No. I think you should talk to her. By the way, how much power do you have now?"

"Enough."

"She has something you should see."

"Why?"

"It's pretty incriminating."

"Of who?"

"Among others, a prominent politician."

"Them shites! What do you want me to do with it?"

“Make sure it is seen by those who can make sure justice is done.”

Setanta looked hard at Quirk who sat looking out of the window. They had fought each other, these two, almost down to the last man on each side but they knew that, however irreconcilable their differences were, they both shared the same vision of what constituted a just society. Like warriors before and since, they were innately-conservative men who both subscribed to minimum but fair governance. They shared the same vision for Ireland too, under the bombast and political mismanagement on both sides that made them cringe. When a political solution *was* obtained or negotiated, they were willing to support it but they expected the politicians to obey the spirit as well as the letter of any agreement but were invariably disappointed. Having spent and shed blood in their espoused cause, they expected such solutions to be respected, even in compromise for which, as pragmatists, they saw the need. Long in the tooth and long in the service of a fervent nationalism which was identical deep under the surface, they perhaps had had enough of fighting and had sweet dreams of a contented retirement among their roses and friends. Families had never been on either of their agendas and at this moment they were regarding each other with an emotion which they would have fervently denied because it was embarrassingly close to friendship.

“All right. I’ll get it into the right hands,” said Setanta. He pressed a buzzer on his desk and the door opened.

“Bring me the woman,” he said to Crewcut who stood there. He then walked to a cupboard against the wall and opened it. There were several bottles and glasses in it. He turned to look at Quirk.

“I always wondered if you were a whiskey or a brandy man.”

“I’m surprised it’s not in your files. I know that you’re a Paddy man.”

"Do you now? Will you join me?"

"I will, if there's no Powers."

Setanta poured two generous tots of Paddy whiskey into two glasses and brought them back to the desk. They nodded at each other in a half-hearted toast and sipped silently.

33

Kitty came out of her doze at the sound of the door opening. Crewcut stood there. He nodded his head over his shoulder and half turned away. She rubbed her eyes, ran her hands through her hair and followed him out into the corridor. He walked away and she followed. Further down they passed an open door and she glanced in as she passed. What she saw made her stop suddenly. The driver was slowly putting on his coat as if he was in pain. His face was swollen and bruised and as he grimaced, she saw his front teeth were missing. He caught her eye and nodded carefully. She took a half pace towards the open door but her arm was grabbed quickly and she was pulled along the corridor. She resisted, still looking at the badly-beaten man who shook his head and gestured for her to walk on by. She did so and her arm was released.

She followed her guide in a state of shock. Who were these men? Ever since she was a child, she had known that Irish politics had raised a great deal of ill will among several opposing interest groups; nationalistic against loyalist; moderate against extremist, Catholic against Protestant, Protestant sect against Protestant sect. It had been tiresome but now the danger of it came home to her. It was bad enough being swept up in the criminal acts that Tomas had unearthed but this development upped the stakes and made her feel very insecure indeed. They arrived at a double door, which Crewcut opened and stepped aside. She went in and the relief when she saw Quirk was almost overwhelming.

"Mr Quirk. Where am I?" she blurted out, close to tears. "Who are these people? Your driver got beaten up. What's going on?"

Quirk rose and came to her. He held both her hands and led her to the chair he had just vacated.

"Sit down, Kitty," he said. "Everything is going to be all right. This is Setanta."

The relief gave way to anger. Her hands started to tremble and she gripped the sides of her blouse. Her broken nail snagged in the material and she let rip.

"So you're responsible for all this?" she cried. "I came here because I was told I could trust you and what happened? You beat up the person who drove me here and you lock me in a room with two gorillas."

"I can understand your anger—" Setanta started.

"No you can't! You can't understand my fucking anger because you're used to this sort of brutality and I'm not. I thought up until now that I lived in a country where the rule of law protected me from the likes of you."

"The rule of law," said Setanta, unruffled. "which you take so much for granted, I have found to be a very fragile thing. So fragile that it takes perpetual vigilance on the part of the likes of me to keep it in place. However, it's not the time to discuss such things. You have something you wish me to see."

She sat there seething, glaring at this imperturbable man. Quirk coughed quietly.

"Kitty," he said. "He's right. And he can help you. He may be the only man in Dublin who can show what you have to people who can do something about it. Let's talk about what you have."

"But your driver? He was badly beaten."

"He's been beaten before. It comes with the job."

"What job?"

"That's none of your business," she was taken aback at his tone.

"Well?" Setanta asked quietly.

"Are you on the web?" Kitty asked. "I can download it."

Without a word he entered some commands on the computer and stood up and away from the desk. Kitty took his seat and studied the screen. The home page was one of the more powerful search engines. She typed in the URL that Jack had made her memorise and his home page filled the screen. She clicked on the 'Archive' button and input her code when requested. She typed 'Kitty' in the window and sat back as the tape started to download. Setanta had a powerful server and plenty of bandwidth so the file was downloaded in moments. She hit play and stood up. Setanta and Quirk came around the desk and watched in silence as the scene with Curran, O'Shea and Dougherty unfolded.

There was silence when it finished. Kitty broke it.

"My brother made that tape. Curran killed him or had him killed."

"Can you prove that?" Setanta asked.

"John-Joe Crosby overheard them discussing the killing and passing over a bribe. He'll swear to it."

"I took a sworn affidavit from John-Joe," said Quirk.

"Where would Curran be now?" asked Setanta. Quirk looked at his watch.

"He'll be at Arena21 in an hour or so?"

Setanta pressed a buzzer under his desktop. The door opened immediately and Crewcut stepped in.

"Ten men. Armed. And get me a judge. I'll need a warrant."

"Yesss!" said Crewcut as he walked out. Setanta looked at Kitty.

"Is there a nail file in this kip?" she asked.

34

For the Kerry team, the night before the match was fraught with tension and irritability. Over a modest supper, the Kerry players were rude to Quirk's men who gave as good as they got and by the time they left the table, John-Joe was in despair at the complete lack of mutual tolerance. He and Tim had considerable trouble getting them into the main conference room where McGarrity had arranged to talk to them about teamwork and motivation. John-Joe was sceptical as to the likely success of that. He didn't think McGarrity's avuncular style would resonate with his gang of barely-controlled anxious, nervous, insecure and tense men his team had turned into as soon as they had arrived in Dublin. The extensive coverage the *Danann* (more than the Kerry team) had garnered on the television channels and the social media hadn't helped. He knew that they were close to being overwhelmed by the atmosphere on the eve of the most brutal match they were ever faced with. It had been decided that contact with family and friends would be severed for the twenty-four hours preceding the conflict and John-Joe was now having second thoughts as to the advisability of that. Little personal expressions of love and support would have helped diffuse the situation, he thought.

McGarrity had disagreed so vehemently that he had swept all before him. Now, he was going to show them a movie! Jesus! These were men. Mature and capable enough to be in the right mind to play the way they knew they had to. McGarrity had disagreed with that too, explaining patiently that the toughest military forces in the USA, were fed a diet of Hollywood's best war movies before a tough operation and invariable absorbed sufficient quantities of testosterone-laden imagery to carry them on to the heights of bravery, team spirit and determination. But McGarrity had also strongly advised that the Kerry team were not to tackle the *Danann* on their own – brutal – terms. So what was the film going to be? Some sort of heart-warming schmaltz about the brotherhood of man? He knew he was being unfair to a very intelligent and insightful man but still he worried.

Inside the bug-proof room the men settled down as McGarrity stood, head bowed at the front, his hands clasped behind his back. He kept this pose until the men settled down, unsure of what was coming. When the tension had become embarrassing, he lifted his head and surveyed the men.

"The *Danann* will play the man. Every time. You will play the ball. That's how you will win."

He knew that he had fed directly into their fears of the formidable men they were about to face and he let them dangle a while in the imagery he knew was running through their minds. They knew all the *Danann*. Had studied their records, the assessments of them and their style of play, and their fears were by no means allayed.

"You have studied the *Danann*." Almost all of them nodded. "Seen them in action. Analysed their moves. You think you know them well enough to face them tomorrow?" Not all of them nodded this time. John-Joe stood to one side, looking at their faces, wondering where this was going to lead. They were wondering too.

"Well, here are some images of the *Danann* which you have

not seen. Look at them well. They will alter your image of these hairy-arsed hooligans – forever."

He snapped his fingers and an image came on the screen that silenced them all. It was a beautifully drawn cartoon of Vinnie in full *Danann* regalia, wielding a hurley and galloping towards a line of green-shirted players who stood between him and a goal. It was a two-dimensional cartoon, superbly drawn and the music and sound effects were a mix between Hanna Barbera's *Tom and Jerry* shorts and Spike Jones. Slavering at the mouth, Vinnie reached into his shorts and hauled out a monstrous set of genitalia. Grabbing one of the swollen testicles, he bounced it up and down on his hurley as he ran. The other testicle dangled and jangled to and fro beneath the hurley. The audience in the room started to laugh as Vinnie flicked the testicle up into the air and dealt it a tremendous whack with the hurley. It and the dangling testicle sped towards the goal as the line of green-shirted defenders parted in fear. The testicles sped on, the intervening pouch of the scrotum started to spin, turning the forward movement into that of a pair of bolas. As it approached the goal, it slowed down just before the goal line. The scrotum and the tissue that connect it to the still captive and engorged penis – shown in a quick cut-away – started to contract and the scrotum and the two testicles still spinning, whipped back to where they had been launched – and connected with a stunned Vinnie, wrapping themselves around his neck as he fell to the ground. As he gagged and gurgled, his penis emitted spouts of white matter over the field. The screen went blank and the audience was in stitches, rolling on the floor and thumping each other in delighted amazement.

"That cartoon and more like it were launched onto almost all social media platforms early this morning and already millions of responses, almost all favourable, have been rolling in. We even managed to intrude this one onto the *Danann* website. Needless to say, it was whipped off very quickly but not before it had been seen and passed on."

McGarrity screened several more such cartoons showing various members of the *Danann* in hilarious situations, including scatological, and the Kerry team loved them.

"Curran has increased the newsworthiness of these by trying to sue the perpetrators and, with luck, he will resort to the courts, thus increasing the exposure immeasurably," McGarrity continued. "We will also broadcast them as static images on the mobile devices we have on our records immediately prior to the match tomorrow. I daresay they will be blocked inside the stadium but not before some of the spectators will have accessed them and you will be informed. I suggest that you greet the *Danann* with disdainful laughter. A few rude gestures from you will not go amiss. The point of this exercise is to undermine the effect of their dramatic entry. It will get their collective goats and hopefully throw them off their strides. And now, I want you to view a film, one made in the 1960s about one man who tackled the whole world, a slave called Spartacus. And here's an interesting thing about this movie. A blacklist existed in Hollywood at that time that forbid the hiring of any writer who had a record of having belonged, however casually, to the Communist Party and believe me, with America in severe depression and with millions of men out of work and out of hope, there were a lot of communists or what they called 'fellow travellers' around. One such was a great movie writer called Dalton Trumbo and, against the strictures of the studio bosses, Kirk Douglas who owned the rights and who was the studio's biggest star, insisted on getting Trumbo to write the script. A job Trumbo enjoyed immensely. You might find it a little old fashioned at first but I assure you it is well worth watching."

The lights dimmed and the Stanley Kubric film *Spartacus*, with Kirk Douglas in the role, started. At first its measured pace and slightly-hokey situations elicited a few guffaws from the team but gradually the strong story and the superb cast of actors wove their spells and the men were hooked. As Spartacus dies on the cross at the end and Jean Simmons bids him a desolate farewell, a few furtive fingers wiped a few furtive tears away before the lights were turned on again. The men quietly filed out in a sombre mood but John-Joe, who was standing at the door, saw that they had been profoundly moved and had related to the glorious futility of the protagonist's struggle. "dammit' he thought. McGarrity was right. Again.

35

Curran knew that the crowd was as much interested in the staging of the match as the match itself. So the musical acts before the entry of the teams were the best that money and busy international schedules could accommodate. Heavy metal was the order of the day and it served to prime the emotions of the crowd for some brutal, visceral action. The group's percussion and pounding, savage chords appealed to the younger people present – and there were plenty of those. The older, more-traditionally-inclined people were, however, offended by the cacophonous assault on their ears and by the time the three, seemingly interminable, sets were finished, the edge of expectation had been blunted somewhat, although the reaction on the internet which Curran was carefully monitoring was all that he could have asked for. It was a flood of highly-appreciative comments although a careful analysis of the demographics of the respondents was less reassuring. The respondents were young, very young, well below marriage age, voting age, drinking age and those arbitrary barriers which various societies are inclined to impose on their young, in an effort to keep them away from 'harmful' influences. When this was pointed out to Curran by a nervous and diffident communications manager, he was taken aback but recovered and exclaimed that he was already building future audiences for the game. But inwardly, alarm bells were ringing.

The sheer drama of the entry of the *Danann* team altered the entire mood. From an invisible grid of wires above the pitch, each team member descended in an enveloping wisp of translucence material that shimmered and crackled in beams of ultraviolet light. As each player landed on the field, he was greeted by a beautiful young girl in a diaphanous gown who handed him his hurley and took away the shimmering cocoon. The players marched proudly to their positions and waited silently. The *Danann* anthem played through all of this but such was the visual effect that the music did not have the intended emotional impact, a fact that did not escape Curran. The team was greeted by a roar but to his well-attuned ear, it was nowhere as loud or as excited as at the first match. He was convinced, however, that the entry of the Kerry team would be an embarrassing anti-climax. Quirk and John-Joe had insisted that they manage the entry and they wanted no effects, merely the playing of their chosen anthem.

After a few suitably dramatic moments of silence, a section of ground at the end of the pitch rose up, as it had at the inaugural game and the pure, opening chords of the Irish National Anthem, *Amhrán na bhFiann*, rang out; a five-chord phrase, C, A, E, A, D, each rendered by different musical instruments, well-tuned kettle drums, a soaring soprano, a pristine violin, a duet of oboes, a trio of trombones and a sextet of trumpets. Each phrase grew bigger and hung in the air as the Kerry team walked out in a very relaxed and casual manner, each in a simple green jersey and white, rather baggy shorts and each clutching his hurley loosely in his hand while looking around at the crowd and waving. As the anthem itself started to play in a dramatic rendering, the crowd joined instantly, the majority of them standing to attention as they sang. There was no ignoring the difference and Curran's normally-impassive countenance clearly showed his anger and displeasure. He passed out instructions for the cameras to focus on the *Danann* team exclusively and the remotely-controlled cameras did just that, but the many camera operators covered the standing crowd and kept the Kerry team centre frame as they calmly walked to their allotted positions and stood facing the *Danann*, until the anthem stopped and the excited and appreciative roar of the crowd filled the stadium. Some internet manipulation ordered by Quirk and cheerfully facilitated by Jack blasted images of the scurrilous *Danann* caricatures onto the platforms of the digital world, even intruding momentarily onto Currans' dedicated netcasts. Each lasted only a second or two but it was long enough to prick the formidable *Danann* image through humour. While that was happening, several of the Kerry team did something that the crowd loved, turning their backs on the *Danann*, they lowered their shorts and exposed their white, well-rounded posteriors to them. The crowd went wild, cheering, laughing and whistling in derision at the highly-discomfited *Danann*.

A countdown clock appeared on each screen and a klaxon blared as the zero was reached. The players ran to take up their positions and a glowing hurling ball was shot from a hidden catapult and landed in the exact centre of the pitch.

The game was on and the crowd soon showed they were on the side of the Kerrymen. With Quirk's men providing a shield between their teammates and the *Danann*, the Kerrymen clawed out room for their brand of classic hurling; deft passes, feints to left and right and devastatingly accurate pucks gave them an edge and they took full advantage of it. The *Danann* took some time to recover from their less than adulatory welcome from the crowd which they had been told would be rooting for them. The crowd certainly wasn't. Each choreographed Kerry move was rewarded by an approving roar and each brutal attack by the *Danann* was greeted by a mixture of approval – and disapproval, something the *Danann* were not used to and did not expect. They were discomfited and thrown off their collective strides. Vinnie was everywhere, cajoling, encouraging and bullying – effectively when he was in the immediate vicinity of some waverers, instantly forgotten when he dashed off to another weakening spot. In this tumultuous situation, it was inevitable that the Kerrymen would score and score they did. An unexpected pass from Tim to right of the field, found three Kerrymen eagerly awaiting. One of them scooped the ball out of the sky and instantly passed it to the second while the third moved confidently towards the *Danann* goal in the firm expectation that the low-flying ball would reach his outstretched hurley. And reach it, it did, so closely that all he had to do was arrest momentarily the forward momentum of the ball, deflect it up to shoulder height and grasping the hurley with both hands, send it screaming at and through the *Danann* goal. The klaxon blared and most of the crowd went wild.

The goal puck sent the ball back to the centre of the pitch where John-Joe was waiting and ready to try the carefully rehearsed Garryowen manoeuvre. It went like clockwork; once he had the ball on his hurley and at his prearranged whistle, Quirk's men formed a wedge with Tim at the apex. John-Joe's pass reached Tim's hurley right on the sweet spot and he charged, tapping the ball up and down as he ran. Quirk's men cut through the speedily assembled *Danann* like a knife through butter. Those *Danann* who tried to cut into the wedge to reach Tim, were swatted aside almost contemptuously by the firmly-held angled hurleys and suddenly the way was cleared to the *Danann's* goal. This time the klaxon for Kerry's second goal was drowned out by the crowd's vociferous approval.

36

In the control box, Curran was livid but, with a great effort, he controlled his temper as he surveyed the monitor screens. They, at least, were reassuring. The worldwide involvement in the game was astounding. Never before had such immediate reactions been generated in such volumes. An interactive programme had been inserted into the broadcast. Thanks to an embedded chip in the ball, each movement in the game was plotted in real time on the screens of participating players. Each player could indicate the likely movement of the ball to any of the hurlers on the screen and if the movement was carried out as indicated, the player received credits which amassed, or decreased, depending on the accuracy of the player's anticipation. Millions of players were participating and the electronic action of the screens was unprecedented. One fact, however, did not fail to be noticed by Curran; the result of the Garryowen manoeuvre had been correctly anticipated by the vast majority of players. If only the *Danann* had been as prescient, he thought.

On the field, Vinnie understood what was happening and he circulated as much as he could, cursing here, encouraging there, bolstering flagging psyches, and assuaging bruised egos.

'Don't worry. They'll wear themselves out. We'll soon have the bastards where they belong.' was the tenor of his remarks and rally them he did. Shame and anger tapped into all the training they had absorbed and collectively they realised that the treatment they were receiving from the Kerrymen was nothing to the chastisement they had received from the trainers at the *Danann* gym. When the ball was again in play, they had recovered their highly-focused determination and by now they had identified the shock players of the Kerry team. Each of them singled out one of Quirk's men as a focus for their raging revenge.

The next stage of the contest was brutal, bloody and merciless. Quirk's men didn't know what hit them. In quick succession and with no regard for the position of, or the possession of the ball, they became the focal point of a pitch of aggression that was all the more victorious because it was relentless. One after another, they were attacked and damaged by hurtling bodies and slashing hurleys. Not being in the vicinity of the ball was no defence. Indiscriminately they were singled out for punishment until even their iron stoicism began to falter. In this miasma of gloom, the *Danann*, perhaps inevitably, scored their first goal.

Having feared that the Danaan would score first, the rest of the Kerrymen concentrated on playing the game according to the ancient rules and in the ancient spirit and, just as succession of single drops of water will wear away the adamantine rock, the skill of the game wore its way into the attention of the spectators off the mayhem and onto the game. Vinnie was the first to perceive the way things were going. He looked hard at the control room above the stands but the toughened glass did not allow the interior to be seen. Turning back to the field which was now strewn by groaning bodies and medical orderlies who were trying to carry them to safety, he whistled shrilly several times and attracted the attention of his team. A few sharp hand signals and a gesture towards the Kerry goal made his intentions clear. He ran to where a Kerryman was about to puck the ball down the pitch and, slamming him to the ground, took possession of the ball. His team were grouped in a formation that they had rehearsed many times in the gym and, scooping up the ball Vinnie ran towards the Kerry goal, the ball bouncing on his hurley. His teammates fell into a prearranged formation on either side of him while two players headed towards the sidelines. When they were in positions that suited Vinnie, he passed the ball to one of his players on his left and headed straight towards the Kerry goal. The chosen player caught the ball and pucked it to one of the sideline players who know exactly what to do, running with the ball until Vinnie smashed his way past two defenders, he pucked the ball ahead of Vinnie who picked up speed, scooped up the ball and sped towards the gaol. Only one Kerry player stood between him and his target and he was dispensed with by a savage chop with Vinnie's hurley held as an axe. The inner, thin edge of the *bas* hit the Kerryman on the collar bone, shattered it and carried on until it broke the shoulder bone and dropped the man. Vinnie didn't break his stride but, moving past the falling man, he positioned himself at an acute angle to the goal and with a graceful, fully-controlled swing of his upper body, sent the ball into the goal. The klaxon for half-time and the roar of the crowd was grim music to his ears.

37

The police van containing Quirk and Kitty moved slowly towards Arena21. Its headlights were out and in the back of the van, two dark-clad men were crouched over a bench crammed with banks of electronic equipment. They both wore headphones and murmured at intervals into throat microphones. The van stopped as the entrance of the stadium came into view. Around the entrance to the arena several uniformed security guards moved to and fro. Kitty spoke first.

"It seems a strange place to arrest him."

"A perfect place. He'll be absorbed in the match and his guard will be down."

"But his men will warn him."

"No, they won't. As soon as Setanta arrives all radio signals on all narrow security channels in the vicinity will be blocked. It won't register on the equipment Curran is using to broadcast the match so he will be totally unaware of our approach." He looked at his watch.

"We'll make our move as soon as Setanta arrives."

"Will he have any problems with the judge?"

"None. He'll be with one of the more… pliable judges here."

"Is there any integrity in this country?"

"Oh yes. There's enough of that. But judges all over the world come from the more, shall we say, conservative ranks of our upper-middle-class society. They are happy, most of the time, to leave matters of national security to people such as us. It's not a matter of integrity, more a matter of appropriately-applied resources. The judges of the world need their Setantas and they give them appropriate elbow room."

"You seem to know a lot about his business. I understood you and he were..."

"On opposite sides? Yes. In a way we are. In another way, we are carbon copies of each other, or were, before things changed up North and I refocused my activities."

"But he hates you, Mr Quirk."

"He hated me just as much as I hated him when we were at loggerheads. Hate, if applied correctly, focusses the mind wonderfully when the stakes are high. When they lessen, the hate does too. It's as if it never was a real emotion, merely a convenient frame of mind."

"That's so cynical!"

"Yes. We are cynics, Setanta and I, insofar as we are highly suspect of ease and wealth because these diminish a nation. That was the philosophy of the ancient cynics, one of whom used to walk around with a lantern in daylight, saying he was looking for an honest man. The modern debasement of the word accuses us of denying sincerity and goodness. Not so. We are merely highly suspicious of those who proclaim themselves as sincere and good. Like Curran. He claims he is preserving the spirit of ancient Ireland, while he is merely abasing a great sport for his own personal enrichment."

Kitty was somewhat out of her depth but she carried on gamely.

"So it's a sort of intellectual game for both of you. It has nothing to do with... patriotism—"

"Which is the last refuge of a scoundrel. In fact, Miss Ring it is *all* about patriotism – what Setanta and I think and do. We both have an image of Ireland which, for all its faults, is one worth preserving. He from the South, me from the North, we both want to protect a collection of people on a small piece of land that has given a lot to the world of what is worth preserving because it is unique, to our binding history, or diverse divisions, to our aggravating differences. We – he and I – are Ireland, warts, idiosyncrasies and all. That's why we fought each other and that's why we are fighting Curran, the great Satan, because he would make us what we are not."

Kitty thought Quirk was mad but of course that wasn't the sort of thing you said to Quirk.

"So what do we do now?" she asked.

"We wait."

Quirk took a silver hip flask out of his pocket and opened it. A strong smell of whiskey filled the car. He offered the flask to Kitty.

"Here. It'll settle your nerves."

Kitty took the flask and downed a generous mouthful. She gasped but immediately felt better.

38

Inside the Kerry team's rest room, John-Joe was addressing the remainder of his players. Their mood varied from man to man. Some of Quirk's men were almost growling with repressed rage and anger and were barely listening to John-Joe. The rest displayed behaviour that ranged from jubilation to fear; some were looking blankly at the floor, oblivious to what was going on around the, displaying a distancing attitude to the rest, some were white and subject to almost imperceptible bouts of shivering. John-Joe was walking about, physically confronting them all by deliberately standing close in front of them and bending over them until they were forced to look him straight in the face. What he saw didn't reassure him. Most of them were on the edge, ready to crack. Gone was the casual confidence they had demonstrated when they first walked out onto the pitch. It was time to remind them what support they had out there. John-Joe signalled to a technician who was standing at a video console at the back of the room. The man pressed some buttons and images appeared on the large TV screen on the wall.

McGarrity had planted several people in the crowd with instructions to interview those in the crowd who were Kerry supporters and record them on mobile devices linked straight to the restroom and independent of any official TV feeds controlled by Curran. Now on the screen quick snippets of people appeared in quick succession. All the interviewees were excited, some were ecstatic, all were supportive;

"Wonderful. Wonderful how those Kerrymen are giving them shit."

"It serves those *Danann* right! Take over our game would they? Well they better learn how to play it first, the bastards."

"Skill will out. It'll win the day. Those Kerrymen are playing like giants."

"Demons! They're wicked! That's what I call hurling! Ireland should be proud of Kerry. I know I am. Did you see that John-Joe score? Brilliant! That bastard Vinnie will be carried off – balls and all! Two to one! They'll wipe the pitch with them before the game is over."

The admiration, even adulation was manifest. The players were drawn out of their distracted states and began to respond with grins of shy pride. They all sat up straighter and even began to snigger and laugh. John-Joe let this mood grow before he spoke.

"So. The crowd is more and more on our side. The *Danann* have been cut down to size – and we're winning. How about that? Did you think, a month, even a week ago, that we could do that? Did you? Did you?"

The returning pride was tangible and even the dour Quirk men were preening.

"We're doing more than saving this match. We're saving the game. No matter how much money Curran throws at his style and no matter how many followers he gets, our style of hurling will continue, stronger than ever." It was time to put on the brakes and bring them back to earth.

"But it's by no means over yet. There's a second half to play and be sure that the *Danann* are getting the same sort of winding up. By now they'll be furious, they'll be made to feel ashamed by Curran, they'll be out to win at any cost."

He paused and watched their euphoria dissipate before he went on.

"And that'll be our opportunity. They'll be reckless and instead of learning from the first half, they will go back to their arrogant ways as soon as they come out. Right now they are rejecting the idea that a Kerry team can conceivably beat them at what they think is their own game. So watch for their weaknesses. Take advantages of the chances they are going to take. Be ready to duck and weave. Remember what Li drummed into us all; the supple, bending reed in the flood, the open hand, not the fist. These are not fancy phrases. These are the facts of this next half and if – no – *when* we win we will not have to play like this ever again. We'll go back to the old style, the classic style that made this game the finest in the world."

The images on the screen suddenly stopped and, with a crackle of snow, the screen went dead. Then the official *Danann* website came on. It extolled the game in glowing terms and John-Joe wanted it off – fast.

"Turn that off. What happened to the interviews?"

"Not sure," said the technician, fiddling with the controls. It's just – hell, my mobile is off.'

"So's mine," said several others in the room.

"What's going on?" asked Tim.

"Doesn't matter," replied John-Joe. "We're back on shortly. Let's concentrate on how we're going to behave."

The team was looking at him with so much trust, he was scared.

"OK. Close your eyes. Breathe deep."

39

One of the dark-clad men in the back of the van swore.

"We're down. You?"

Quirk looked at the blank screen of his mobile phone.

"He's here. He loves an entrance."

Another van pulled up beside them and Setanta got out. He was followed by several dark-clad men. From the other vans more men piled out. Quirk and Kitty emerged from their van and stood waiting.

"Why did you bring her?" asked Setanta.

"I have a feeling she will come in useful."

Setanta glared at her for a moment.

"Besides, I need a nail file."

"Keep out of the way," Setanta snarled and headed towards the stadium entrance where the security guards were milling about and shaking their phones and walkie talkies. They were buzzing with puzzlement as Setana stepped out of the gloom and stood facing them on the pavement, surrounded by his dark-clad men. They were all on rubber soles and moved like wraiths. Setanta held aloft a badge in one hand and a gun in the other.

"Security and Intelligence, Garda Síochána. I have a warrant to enter these premises with the intention of arresting some personnel. I advise you to surrender your weapons and step aside. Anyone who doesn't will feel the full force of these men of mine."

Since all Setanta's men wielded serious automatic and semi-automatic weapons, the guards did not need any further persuasion. Some tried surreptitiously and in vain to activate their phone, the rest held their hands up and were very quickly and professionally lined up facing the wall, deprived of their weapons and their hands bound their hands with plastic wrist ties. Setanta waited until they were all secured and then addressed the man with the most impressive epaulettes.

"You in charge?" The man nodded. "OK, take me to where Curran is right now and walk quietly. No gesturing. No noise. Just get us past any other guards there may be between us and him. Got it?"

With the guard leading the way, they were allowed into the stadium, past a few bemused staff members who were quickly rounded up and secured. The guard led them along the gloomy backs of the stands to where a staircase led from another more discreet entrance, up into the gloom. From here on up the floor was carpeted, the walls panelled and the lighting subdued and soft, obviously a VIP route. Setanta sent four of his men ahead and they ascended the stairs in standard, battle formation pairs, each covering the other as they made short forward movements alternatively. Four other men followed closely behind, ready to deploy as required. There were guards stationed along the route they took but most of them had positioned themselves where they could see the action of the field, at which their full attention was focussed. A swift blow to the head with a rifle butt, followed by deftly applied wrist ties and they were secured. After several short advances, one of the lead men stopped at a corner and signalled Setanta to approach. The last stretch of stairs led up to a small balcony and a set of double doors. Two guards were pacing to and fro in a brighter pool of light.

Setanta stepped back and signalled for Kitty to approach, which she did hesitantly. He gestured at the corner and she peered around it. These guards looked very attentive. Setanta pulled her back and put his mouth close to her ear.

"Distract them," he whispered.

Kitty hesitated and then hiccupped so loudly that Setanta stiffened. But before he could react, Kitty stepped around the corner and said just as loudly; "Is there a nail file anywhere in this fucking kip?" The two men at the door became fully alert as she came into view, staggering slightly. She hiccupped again and moved unsteadily towards them. Behind her, Setanta rolled his eyes at Quirk who shrugged and stifled a grin. The two foremost policemen crouched alertly at the corner, each handing their semi-automatics to a colleague.

Kitty moved towards the stairs in an exaggerated, and stately walk.

"Ahh," she said. "This looks fucking promising."

The two guards exchanged amused looks but didn't relax their guard significantly. Kitty started up the stairs and one guard stepped down to confront her.

"I'm sorry Madame. Guests only."

Kitty drew herself up to her full height and, since she stood on a step lower then him, this brought her face level with his solar plexus.

"I'll have you know that I am a guest. A guest of Mr Curran. I arrived an hour ago but I broke this fucking nail and went to look for a nail file." She leaned towards his breastbone and, holding up her broken nail said confidentially; "There isn't a nail file anywhere in this fucking – oops." She had thought it was time to stagger and stagger she did, falling up a step and past him before she fell on her back, giggling. The guard grabbed her nearest arm but she flopped on down. He sighed and looked at his mate who joined them, grabbed her other arm and tried to get Kitty to her feet. But one of the games Kitty had played with Tomas when they were children was 'floppy doll' when each would lie on the ground and try to prevent the other from lifting them by being as floppy as possible. So Kitty was the Queen of Flop and acted as if each of her limbs was connected to its joint with very old rubber bands. Swearing under their breaths, the two guards were so concentrated on getting this drunken, whiskey-smelling bitch up and the hell out that neither of them felt the blow that compressed the neck nerves so rapidly that they lost consciousness in mid swear.

Quickly Setanta moved up to the door, while the two guards were being secured and gagged. He waited until four of his men were correctly positioned around the door and then reached for the door handle.

He stopped that movement as a loud crash came from behind the door, followed by several voices raised in angry dispute.

40

The second half was well underway, with only twelve men on the field. The mayhem of the first half had accounted for the rest who had been carried off by the medical orderlies. By an unspoken agreement the focus of the match had been reduced down to John-Joe and Vinnie who manoeuvred against each other while the balance of each team concentrated on protecting their captains. The match had deteriorated down to the level of pure tactical defence which would have been mind-numbingly boring to watch – if it were not for the tension as the two main agonists moved warily around the pitch looking for an opening. John-Joe tuned all his facilities on the positioning of Tim and how he could take advantage of it. Tim's nerves were stretched so tight that he felt he could see into John-Joe's mind and he watched his movements like a hawk. Even an almost casual swing of an opposition hurley didn't distract him. He merely deflected it with ease and, turning the hurley in his hand until the sharp point of the bas was facing outwards, he applied a chop on the *Danann*'s patella which shattered knee and brought the *Danann* down, grimacing in agony. Then Tim saw John-Joe take an angled run towards the side of the opposing *Danann*, away from Vinnie. Knowing, from their many years of playing together, what was in John-Joe's mind, Tim ran towards Vinnie, all his nerves strained to anticipate John-Joe's move accurately. John-Joe's puck sent the ball towards a part of the pitch ahead of him and beyond Vinnie. Tim went hurtling towards the spot where the ball would land, concentrating on computing the ball, as it bounced forward and the angle between his approach and the *Danann* goal. He had he math and the momentum firmly in mind as he reached the ball. Going into a well-practiced upward swing of his body, he flicked the ball off the ground and, as it appeared between his eyes and the Danaan goal, he grasped the hurley in both hands and braced himself for the puck. This brought his head back and exposed his neck beneath the grid on his helmet. Vinnie had catapulted his body into position on the side of Tim away from his fast-accelerating hurley and the perfectly-positioned ball. The sharp inner edge of Vinnie's hurley *bas* connected with Tim's windpipe, crushing it beyond repair and severing both carotid arteries and sending such a traumatic signal to his brain that Tim's body stopped functioning and the momentum of his speed brought it crashing to the ground. He was dead before his body stopped sliding.

With an ear-splitting roar of gleeful triumph, Vinnie scooped up the ball and headed towards the Kerry goal, the remaining men in his team instinctively surrounding him in a protective wedge as he sped towards the Kerry goal, his men savagely swatting the Kerrymen aside with lethal blows of their hurleys.

John-Joe knew that Tim was dead. He could almost feel his absence in his mind, so he suppressed his grief and concentrated all his not-inconsiderable power, magnified by an anger and rage that he had never experienced before, on getting to Vinnie. Attacking the *Danann* wedge from behind, he wielded his hurley with grim-and-focussed fury on each *Danann* as he caught up with him. They fell like limp grain before his man-killing sickle until there was nothing between him and the fast-moving Vinnie but a dim mist of hate. Somehow or other a rational part of his brain kicked into gear and reversing his hurley as he approached Vinnie from behind, he brought the tip into sharp and explosive contact with the handle of Vinnie's hurley, which flew from his hand, out of the clutches of his powerful fingers and through the air, tumbling as it went. The ball lost it forward momentum and fell to the ground. Without losing a step, Vinnie threw himself after the hurley reaching for it with both hands. As he stooped to gather it up, John-Joe's feet landed on his kidneys with a pain he had never experience before. He went tumbling to the ground, his arms still outstretched, fingers groping. John-Joe's hurley, wielded like an axe, descended on Vinnie's shoulder, with all John-Joe's strength and momentum behind it. The axe demolished the shoulder and collapsed the lung and Vinnie, in an agony spasm, turned over and lay, gasping up at John-Joe who was raising his hurley over his head for a *coup de grace*. Then, unexpectedly, he grinned and spoke in a hoarse whisper.

"You like it, don't you, you fucking Kerry bastard. Beats your style of hurling, hey?"

Blood came bubbling out of his mouth and, spitting it out, he went on.

"You'll win the match, you piece of shit. But you'll lose the war."

The crowd was hushed, mesmerised by the gladiatorial tableaux; the man on the ground, the victor poised over him, hurley raised. John-Joe slowly lowered his hurley and went over to scoop up the ball. He returned to where Vinnie lay and placed the ball on Vinnie's feebly moving breast. Then he appraised the *Danann* gaol. Also in his line of sight, was the command post, suspended over the seats at the corner of the field. He positioned himself next to Vinnie and grasped his hurley firmly. Then bending his body in a graceful arc, he flicked the ball off

Vinnie's breast, drew back the hurley – and sent the ball at the window of the command post, behind which he knew Curran was watching his dreams of physical and moral superiority fade away.

The silicon-based polymer laminate on the glass of the window slowed the ball slightly but its main function was to provide some resistance to the hardened glass beneath. This glass flattened the ball and absorbed the energy of its forward motion. In doing so it shattered but the inner laminate deformed and absorbed the remainder of the energy and prevented the glass from entering the command post. The ball dropped away, the window remained – barely – in place and the crowd went wild.

41

The sight that confronted Setanta as he entered, gun at the ready, gave him pause. The large window overlooking the pitch was shattered. In front of it stood Curran, his shoulders shaking and his clenched fists beating against his thighs. There were several other men in the room among whom Setanta recognised Dougherty who had quickly collected himself and was sidling towards the door. A quick gesture from Setanta sent one of his men to intercept him and he stood there, sweating. Curran turned away from the window and was beckoning at one of his security men when he saw Setanta standing there, wielding a gun and reaching into his breast pocket. Curran froze and cleared his throat. The voice that came out was not his usual clipped and confident one.

"W… what do you want? How dare you burst in here? This—"

"Mr Charles 'Jack' Curran, I have three warrants of arrest here. One is for you, the second is for Mr Patrick O'Shea and the third is for Teachtaí Dála Eamon Dougherty there. None of you are obliged to say anything unless you wish to do so, but whatever you say will be taken down in writing and may be given in evidence."

Another gesture sent two of his men towards those named and started to secure their wrists behind them. Curran found his voice.

"This is totally unacceptable!" he barked. "I refuse—"

A middle-aged man in the group stood and coughed warningly.

"Mr Curran. Please say nothing. This can – and will be – sorted out. Whoever you are, I am Mr Curran's lawyer and any questions must be addressed through me. Here is my card."

Setanta ignored the card and handed the documents to the lawyer.

"You'll find these in order. We will converse in my office."

He nodded at his men and strode out of the door. The arrested men were ushered out and Kitty ran towards the window. What she saw there made her gasp and tears rushed to her eyes.

On the pitch, John-Joe had lifted the body of Tim in his arms and was walking around the perimeter of the pitch. The few Kerrymen remaining were walking behind him, hurleys held aslant ahead of them. As they passed in front of the seats, the crowd rose to its collective feet and bowed their heads. A confused cacophony rose from the rest of the crowd and the cameras, left to the discretion of the individual operators, zoomed in on him. He paused at the entrance to the rest-rooms tunnel and cleared his throat.

"This…" his voice was a croak. He took a deep breath and started again and everyone in the stadium and every watcher around the world clung onto each word as his voice grew stronger. "This—" he raised Tim's body up to his chest. "This is no price to pay for a sport. Any sport."

He blinked away the tears and headed towards the tunnel where he could see Kitty waiting for him. Some unknown operator activated the sound system and the strains of the National Anthem came out loud and proud. The few still seated in the crowd rose to their feet and as the lyrics started, they all joined in;

Sinne Fianna Fail, ata faoi gheall ag Eirinn
Buion dar slua, thar toinn do rainig chugainn.

42

"So they hung Dougherty out to dry?"

"Not before time, the slitherer. He's been getting away with murder for a long time. Another one?"

Quirk nodded and slid his glass across the desk. He and Setanta were demolishing a bottle of Paddy whiskey in Setanta's office.

"And O'Shea?"

"He's just one of Curran's many minions. Not important."

"Do you think Curran will sit?"

"Probably. But he has so many bloody lawyers on the job, it'll take 'til the second coming."

"And his game?"

"Your guess is as good as mine."

Quirk sipped his refreshed drink and looked into the amber liquid for a moment before he replied.

"I believe it will play itself out. Find its… niche, they call it, like reality television, Pacman, Pokémon, *pogue mo thoin*. Do you remember the hula hoop?"

"I do. Didn't the whole world throw its back out with that?"

"They all had their day. The new style will carry on, with its own audience. The important thing is that it has been sidelined. There's always a market for brutality in a so called stable society." Meantime, the old style will carry on and there's talk of it becoming an Olympic sport."

Setanta played with his drink.

"The score didn't matter at all, did it?"

"Not a bit. That wasn't the point," Quirk sighed. "And all those fine young men. They'll never play again."

"Some of your men were hurt."

"They're used to it, like your men. The young hurlers didn't know what hit them."

"I hear John-Joe has given up the game."

"Not really. He's gone away to lick his wounds and mourn his pal."

"Thanks to you."

"It's the least I could do. I was partly responsible for sending him after Curran and after the funeral, he and Kitty got together and they both deserved a decent honeymoon."

"Will he ever play again, do you think?"

"He's sort of committed to training when he comes back and I'm sure the call of the caman will work its magic."

"Why were you so against the new style, anyway? You have always dealt in violence?"

"It's not the violence. I've seen worse, ordered worse—"

"And committed worse."

"Surely. That too. But if there is anything worth preserving in this land of pygmies, it's hurling."

There was another long pause before Quirk spoke; "Do you remember all those old stories? The great heroes, the great deeds. Didn't you want to be one of the Fianna, the Tuatha de Danann?"

"Why do you think I chose my code name?"

"Setanta. The hound of Cúchulainn. It's apt."

"He became Cúchulainn's dog for a year. I became one for a lifetime."

"Do you regret it?"

"Not really, although I would have wished I did what I did for some band of warriors and not the pasty-faced Dubliners I see about me every day."

"You've not the copyright on pinched faces. We've our share up North. Did you every take cognisance of the pink nostrils of the Irish?"

"Nostrils that never snorted fire."

"Snot's all they're good for."

"John-Joe was cast in the old mould, the heroic one," said Quirk "And Tim. God love him, he loved the bones of John-Joe."

"So was Vinnie. A worthy adversary, he was. Like Goll mac Morna."

Quirk laughed and leaned forward.

"Finn's old enemy. Yes. He was worthy."

There was another long pause and for such hardened men who had lived on the edge all their adult lives, it was a comfortable pause. This time Setanta broke it.

"Nowhere in your files does it say that you're a romantic. I would never have thought it."

"A romantic? I suppose I am in a way. Yeats was a great one for that. He lamented Romantic Ireland and consigned it to O'Leary's grave."

"So here we are, two ould tossers, reminiscing."

"I like to see us as two elders, having a dialogue."

Setanta leaned forward.

"Agallamh na Seanórach," Setanta said. "Yes. The dialogue of the elders. You and me – two old Fenians – all we need is Saint Patrick."

Quirk was also leaning forward.

"Oisin and... What's his name?"

"Caílte. Caílte mac Rónáin. Boasting about Fionn and the Fenians."

"Well it's all done for me now. I retire at the end of the

month, with a gold watch and a pension that won't keep me in Paddy."

"What'll you do?"

No idea. This..." Setanta looked around at the skimpy furnishing, "doesn't prepare you for growing roses."

There was a pause in the conversation while Setanta poured another two drinks and Quirk looked closely at his old-time antagonist. He picked up the glass, nodded his thanks and suddenly said.

"Join me."

Setanta replaced his glass on the desk and looked at Quirk.

"Join you?"

"Why not? There's still work to be done. Not here. This place is settled – for the moment. There are other countries, other wars, other problems to be sorted out."

"Ah, it wouldn't be the same. My heart wouldn't be in it."

"I wouldn't want your heart. Your arse is all I need. The problems are all the same, deep down, everywhere. Somebody has to mind the hens when the foxes are loose."

"It's tempting."

"And all the Paddy you can drink."

They drank to that.